Scary Beautiful

How Not to Spend Your Senior Year
BY CAMERON DOKEY

Royally Jacked
BY NIKI BURNHAM

Ripped at the Seams
BY NANCY KRULIK

Spin Control
BY NIKI BURNHAM

Cupidity
BY CAROLINE GOODE

South Beach Sizzle
BY SUZANNE WEYN AND DIANA GONZALEZ

She's Got the Beat
BY NANCY KRULIK

30 Guys in 30 Days
BY MICOL OSTOW

A Novel Idea
BY AIMEE FRIEDMAN

Animal Attraction
BY JAMIE PONTI

Scary Beautiful

NIKI BURNHAM

Simon Pulse
New York London Toronto Sydney

SIMON PULSE
An imprint of Simon & Schuster Children's Publishing Division
1230 Avenue of the Americas, New York, NY 10020
Copyright © 2006 by Nicole Burnham
All rights reserved, including the right of reproduction in whole or in part in any form.
SIMON PULSE and colophon are registered trademarks of Simon & Schuster, Inc.

Designed by Ann Zeak
The text of this book was set in Garamond 3.

Manufactured in the United States of America
First Simon Pulse edition January 2006
10 9 8 7 6 5 4 3 2 1

Library of Congress Control Number 2005927686
ISBN-13: 978-0-689-87619-6
ISBN-10: 0-689-87619-X

For my brother Chuck,
Super Runner of the Universe

One

No one will admit it, but the first day of school rocks. Not the starting classes or getting loaded with homework part of it (please). It's the seeing everyone again part. It's getting all the gossip on who hooked up or broke up, who went on cool vacations to Maui (preferably sans parents) or had cat fights at sports camp. And—best of all—it's trying to predict which of the quiet, semi-invisible girls got a dye job, lost weight, or nabbed some fantastic summer gig in Paris and will therefore be angling to move into the "in" crowd.

My friends and I are always as hot to guess who'll be the year's surprise social superstar as my dad is to bet his retirement fund on whatever new-ish company he thinks will be the Next Big Thing on Wall Street.

Conversely, my friends and I also like to speculate about who'll fall on their face, becoming the pariah of the year. It's never a nice thing to see happen, but such is life.

This year, though, I'm too depressed to notice any of the usual first day of school maneuvering, even though everyone around me seems electrified with the possibilities of the year ahead.

The reason why is simple. Sean's not here.

Sean Norcross and I have been together since roughly halfway through eighth grade (okay, there's no "roughly" about it—it's been ever since he kissed me at exactly 7:48 p.m. on January 10, while standing in the snow in the parking lot after the school talent show.) So starting junior year with him all the way across the country sucks.

I mean, who in their right mind moves from Vista Verde, Colorado, all the way to New Haven, Connecticut, when they have three kids in high school? Well, that's just what Professor and Mrs. Norcross did. Sean's dad accepted a job teaching at Yale, since apparently the Ivy League's more fulfilling professionally than the University of Colorado. The Allied van left a month ago, headed east on I-70 with all the Norcrosses' furniture and at least a dozen boxes full of Professor Norcross's books on molecular biology. However, Sean, his younger brother, Joe, and his older sister, Darcy, were allowed to stay behind with their next-door neighbors for a couple weeks to finish up their summer jobs and tell everyone good-bye before they started at their uppity new East Coast private high school.

It sucked, seeing his house standing empty like that, knowing Sean was down to his last few days and would be following that bright orange moving van out of town.

Three days before he had to leave, Sean and I looked up New Haven on MapQuest and printed off the driving directions, just for kicks and giggles. I didn't tell Sean, but I wanted to do it just so I could mentally find my way there when I'm trying to go to sleep at night. It's exactly 1,867 miles from Vista

Verde to New Haven, which MapQuest says should take only twenty-eight hours and ten minutes to drive. Even if that time includes bathroom breaks and stops for gas, it's a long haul.

Although counting miles is probably as good as counting sheep when I need to get myself to sleep, seeing that distance all plotted out on paper made me feel like I wasn't about to lose an appendage. Like I could draw a line from Point A to Point B and still connect with Sean.

Unfortunately, I was stupid enough to think that Sean would want to try to make it work across that long distance too.

But no. Even if I *could* make that drive to New Haven, there wouldn't be a point. Because when Sean saw that map, it was like a switch flipped in his brain that said, "Babycakes, this relationship is *so over*." Our funky, cool connection, the one that enabled us to find each other instantly on a crowded football field or during a school assembly, no matter what else was happening around us, snapped just like that.

Only I didn't know it.

So this morning, instead of doing my

usual people watching while I stand in junior hall, making mental notes about who's likely to make the cheerleading squad out of nowhere and who's going to wish they were invisible by the end of the month, I'm facing my new locker, messing with a combination lock that doesn't want to work, and I'm about two deep breaths away from tears. Everyone's staring at me as they walk past, and even though I'm used to people staring at me because of how I look, today I just don't want to deal.

I glance at the card with my new locker combo on it again, then try to dial the numbers once more, wishing I could disappear inside my locker, just for a few hours, and stare at nothing but the cold, dark metal.

Then I realize that even doing that won't give me peace. If I get the stupid lock open, it's not like I can put Sean's picture in the back anymore without looking totally pathetic. At least, not once everyone learns that he dumped me cold while having breakfast at Pour la France in the main terminal of DIA, less than an hour before he hopped on the plane.

Who ends a relationship of two and a half years in an airport over scrambled eggs and French toast?

I feel Amy Bellhorn approaching before she speaks, and I will myself not to exude the aura of a red-eyed, horribly depressed dumpee.

"Chloe!"

"Hey!" I turn toward her, trying to sound equally excited. Since she's my best friend, I know how much she loves the first day of school—even more than I usually do. I give her a big happy-first-day-of-junior-year smile before focusing on my locker again. "What do you have first period?" I ask, sounding chipper enough to deserve an Oscar, given how I feel. "I'm in honors English."

"Mr. Whiddicomb or Mrs. Gervase?"

"Whiddicomb. You too?"

"Yep! This rocks. . . . We can catch up. So how'd things go with Sean before he left? Did Darcy and Joe give you any time alone together at the airport? God, you must be missing him like crazy already. I'd have called when I got my class schedule, but I knew you two wanted to spend as much time together as possible and then I was clothes shopping to get ready—"

"Thanks." I haven't told anyone about the breakup yet, not even Amy. I know I'll probably tear up the minute I say Sean's name, and I definitely will once anyone asks the *how did it happen?* question. No way do I want to go on a sniffly, ugly-ass crying jag on the first day of school.

I need to get myself to the point where I can talk about it, at least to Amy, without getting worked up before the first word even leaves my mouth, or else I'm going to be *the* topic of gossip today, and I hate being the focus of people's attention. It gives me the creepy crawlies, even when it's good attention that has nothing to do with my appearance, like when I get a high grade and the teacher puts it on the board, or when I make a killer return during a tennis match.

Amy puts a hand on my arm. "Hey, Chloe, you doing okay?"

Even though I mentally scream out *no*, I give Amy the best smile I can manage. "Okay enough. I think I just need to make it through this first week without him." Really without him.

"I'm here if you need to vent, you know."

I feel my jaw locking, so I just nod.

She apparently gets that it's time to change the subject as I give the lock a final, unnecessarily rough yank, because she tucks a stray strand of hair behind her ear, then pulls her schedule out of a notebook and holds it in front of her. "So let's compare. Who else did you end up with?"

I put a few items from my backpack into the empty steel locker, then pull out the schedule that came in the mail last week and hand it to her. "Pretty much everything I wanted. I ended up with Schneider for chemistry, though. Sixth period."

"Ouch. I managed to get Cooper. Fifth period. Apparently she's only teaching the one chem class this year too."

Lucky her. "That's when I have independent study. It was the only hour where Mrs. Berkowski could sponsor me, so I couldn't change it." I make a face. "Figures that's when Cooper would have chemistry. The one hour I can't be there."

It's not that one teacher's cooler than

8

the other. Mr. Schneider just has a way, way tougher grading curve than Ms. Cooper and everyone knows it. Well, except college admissions officers, which is really the problem.

As we walk toward the gym, where they're having an assembly to update us on all the usual first day of school stuff, Amy stops walking and looks at me. "You know, you really look awesome, Chloe. Cleopatra exotic, you know? Especially since you were out in the sun and got a little more color."

I didn't take any extra time with my hair or clothes today, even though normally I would have because everyone does on the first day back (whether they'll admit it or not), so I just shrug and keep walking. Amy falls in beside me. In an insistent voice, she adds, "No, really. I think you got even better looking over the summer. Like, scary beautiful."

"Oh, please. It's not like you didn't see me all summer. And I know what you're trying to do, so shut up already." I hear the "scary beautiful" thing all the time from Sean. Correction: *used* to hear it all the time from Sean. It was his phrase. I know she's using those exact words to try to make me feel better, but I really don't want to hear it now.

Besides, being pretty got me ostracized back in sixth grade for a while, even though Amy's probably forgotten all about it.

"Remember back when we were in middle school?"

I shoot her a look like, *What, you reading my mind?* but she continues: "On the first day of seventh grade? You hid out in the bathroom before homeroom because you got that awful haircut the day before and you didn't want anyone to see."

"Oh, yeah. Conveniently forgot about that." I told everyone how much I hated that haircut, then went to a different beauty shop the next night and had them recut it so I looked normal again.

What I didn't tell anyone—*especially* Amy—was that I got the bad haircut on purpose, over serious objections from my dad and the horrified stylist.

"Thanks so much for the memory, though," I say as we pass two panicked-looking freshmen. "I'm surprised you didn't take pictures."

"Oh, never," she says, all fake funny, because that's precisely what she did, threatening to publish them in our junior high school yearbook. It was her one and only foray into an organized activity that wasn't sports-related, and she got tossed off halfway through the year for skipping meetings so much. Needless to say, none of her work made it into the seventh grade section.

I wonder sometimes if it would have made things any better for me if she had gotten those pictures printed, just so people could see that I'm not always perfect, that I'm not always pretty, and that I cry over stuff just like anyone else.

Probably not, though. Once people get an impression of you, it's hard to shake. I learned the hard way that getting a bad haircut to make yourself ugly—at least temporarily—isn't enough to do it. The whole episode just ended up making me feel worse.

As we enter the gym and scan the bleachers for open seats in the juniors' section, she says, "Well, I was just thinking things have changed since then, you know?

And how it's a good thing you have a boyfriend, even if he is a zillion miles away. Otherwise, every girl in school would hate you based on looks alone."

Clearly, she doesn't know how much I *don't* want to remember middle school, or she would never say this to me. I mean, I know I'm not ugly, or even average. I have good hair, I'm tall, I don't gain weight easily, and I've never had a single zit. Not a one. It's not that I'm egotistical about it either. It's just a fact of life. A blessing of genetics. And, believe me, pretty girls *know* they're pretty, even the ones who are smart enough to be modest about it and pretend they don't know what they look like.

And I know why they do it. Let me tell you: Pretty sometimes sucks.

I spent nearly all of sixth grade as a pariah to everyone but my very closest friends (and hence the hair-butchering episode to start seventh grade), all because a teacher told me, in front of the whole class, that with my looks I could model. Then— again, in front of the whole class—I was stupid enough to do the polite thing and thank her for the compliment. It was in the context of a Career Day discussion; she'd suggested to a couple people with math smarts that they consider architecture or astronomy, and told my supertalkative friend Rachel that with her people skills, she'd make a great tour guide or party planner.

But the fact that it was a Career Day thing didn't make it any better. I'd been labeled a snob and I was reminded of it every chance my female classmates got, in not-so-polite ways. The cheerleaders were the worst. They'd begged me to go out for cheerleading at the beginning of the year (again, the stereotypical "you're-pretty-you-should-be-a-cheerleader" thing), and when I didn't, they took it as a personal snub, even back then. So they were more than happy to tell everyone I thought cheerleading was beneath me, when the truth is that I'm simply not comfortable in front of crowds. Well, and I can't do a high kick to save my life. My legs just don't go there. And if I tried to do a back hand-spring, I'd probably end up with serious injuries.

I wanted to do it, just to get people to leave me alone. But I didn't have the talent and I knew it.

I know the sometimes-pretty-sucks thing is a minor and probably selfish complaint in comparison to the problems a lot of people have. I mean, I could be dealing with serious issues, like this totally clean girl I know from tennis whose dad keeps getting arrested for drug possession. Or this other girl I know at school whose brother has leukemia. And overall, everyone wants to be good looking, so I guess it's better to be teased about being pretty than about being overweight or having lots of acne or a cartoon voice (though pretty is just as out of my control as those other things are for other people). But for a while there, "pretty" really screwed with my day-to-day life, and it's not like there was anyone I could bitch to about it. You know, the way people always bitch to one another about the little things that annoy them.

Why add to the problem of people thinking I'm stuck-up by complaining to the few friends I still had about being called pretty and stuck-up? Really.

But Sean saved me from all that when he moved here from New Jersey. (Before teaching at CU Boulder, Sean's dad taught at Rutgers.) And for the past two and a half years, I haven't been "pretty Chloe" or "snobby Chloe" in their eyes. I've just been Chloe, the girl who's going out with Sean Norcross, the laid-back, athletic guy everyone likes. And I don't want to go back. Until Amy opened her big mouth, it hadn't occurred to me that it could even be an issue.

You'd think we'd all have matured a little since junior high.

Amy and I climb the bleachers, then shuffle into an open space in the next-to-highest row, just so we can see everything that's going on but not stand out as much as if we were in the top row. Unable to just let it go, I lean over and whisper, "So are you saying that if Sean and I broke up—"

"You're not breaking up!"

"I'm just saying—"

"Then you bet." Amy flips her long, chocolate-colored hair over her shoulders, then gives me a totally wicked grin as if she knows it's never going to happen so she's paying me a huge compliment. "They'd all hate your guts. Just for being your drop-dead gorgeous self. This is the way of the world, O Innocent One."

I feel someone slide into the bleachers on the other side of me. Rachel Nielsen, who also hangs with me and Amy a lot, gives me a quick hug. "How ya doin', Chloe?"

"Fine. Hey, cool shirt." It's pink and floaty without being overdone and it really works with Rachel's short blond hair.

"Thanks. Amy helped me pick it out Saturday afternoon." A guilty look flits over her face, but she quickly covers. "We'd have invited you along, but since Sean was flying out that morning—"

"No problem." Though I vaguely wonder how much they've been doing together this summer while I was wrapped up in spending every possible moment with Sean before he left. For all the good that did.

"I bet you and Sean are missing each other like crazy." Rachel's blue eyes are wide as she says this. "When do you think you'll get to visit?"

I'm about to toss off some noncommittal response, but Amy leans over me. "Rachel, tell Chloe what would happen if she didn't have a boyfriend."

Rachel frowns. "What do you mean?"

I can feel Amy rolling her eyes. "I mean, look at her."

Rachel returns the eyeroll, maybe even exaggerating it. "Oh, *that*. Yeah, every female in school would hate her. Jealous bitches." She smiles at me, as if this is some big inside joke between the two of them, then says, "Whether you'll admit it or not, I know you're probably feeling completely awful with Sean being so far away, but Amy and I'll keep you busy. And you really do look fabulous, so good for you."

I look from Rachel back to Amy. "I know you guys are trying to make me feel better, but I'm really okay. And with the whole people-hating-me thing, you're—"

"Oh no, it's true," Rachel assures me, which makes my stomach sink despite her smile. "But you know we're your buds no matter what."

Rachel leans forward and taps this girl named Alyssa on the shoulder. Alyssa's one of those rare types whom everyone in school likes: smart but not a know-it-all, funny but not obnoxious, decent looking without being too perfect. And she's nice to everyone: the jocks, the super-religious kids, the nerds, the skaters. Even all the self-righteous granolas who wish they went to high school five miles down the road in environmentally conscious Boulder instead of here in Vista Verde, where the real estate's cheaper and their parents can actually afford a house, but where we're not as good about recycling and we have fewer bike lanes. All the kids like Alyssa back, too.

Alyssa looks over her shoulder at Rachel with one of those expressions that shows she's glad to be back at school and catching up on what's what. "Hey, you! Cool top. New?"

"Yeah, thanks. Got it at Colorado Mills over the weekend on sale." Rachel smooths her hands over her denim-clad thighs, then says, "So you're good at reading people, Alyssa. I have an experimental kind of question for you."

I think I'm going to fall through the bleachers, right down to the dust and grime below. I make a face at Rachel, but she doesn't notice or care. And Alyssa looks game, so Rachel continues: "Real quick, without saying her name, think of the girl you despise the most in school."

"I don't really *despise* anyone—"

"Well, one you don't especially like, let's say. Even if it's only in your own mind, and you'd never admit it to anyone. Got it?"

One of Alyssa's dark eyebrows arches up, and I think she's right to be suspicious of Rachel, no matter how cute and blond Rachel may be. "Yeah."

"Is she pretty?"

Alyssa gives a little *harrumph*. "Oh, yeah."

"How pretty? Like, so gorgeous that even if she's complete hellspawn, guys still drool over her for no reason besides her looks?"

"Well, I'm sure they'd claim to be interested in other, um, attributes in her. But—and I won't tell you who she is—I'd say it's all about her looks. Why?"

"Just curious. It's an experiment. Nothing about you specifically. Or whomever you have in mind."

Alyssa seems to accept this. She and

Rachel have known each other since pre-school, so Alyssa's probably used to Rachel firing off wild questions that really don't mean much. She's about to say something else to Rachel, but Principal Orillo takes the microphone and starts tapping it. Alyssa turns around fast so he won't see the back of her head and make an example of her, since he tends to do that. But even though it gets quiet pretty quickly, everyone's still discreetly studying one another, hoping they can get some social insight by memorizing who's sitting with whom.

"You're out of control," I whisper to Rachel.

She whispers back, "Of course!" at the same time Amy whispers, "No, she's just being herself. Running off at the mouth."

For the next forty-five minutes, we listen to Principal Orillo introduce the new staff members and talk about how fabulous the school year will be so long as we all understand the rules and respect each other. Y-a-w-n. He even throws in a cheesy school spirit cheer of "Go, go, Gophers!" (Or, as we like to call ourselves, the Vista Verde Vermin. I mean, get this: Our school color is *green*. Who has a green gopher as a mascot?) After that, the head guidance counselor makes a few announcements about counseling services—both academic and psychological—then we're on our way to morning classes, which will be abbreviated, thanks to the worthless assembly.

"See?" Amy says the second everyone stands up and starts filing out of the bleachers. "I knew Rachel would agree with me that you look great today."

"What, so everyone will hate me?"

"Oh, ignore Rachel," Amy says. "She was trying to make her point. Nobody hates you. But every female in school hates Margot deVries. Even the ones who kiss her ass. If she wasn't so pretty, she wouldn't be so hated. Trust me. You know that's who Alyssa meant, too."

I have to agree. Margot's the type who's always being catty to other girls for her own personal amusement. Her particular forte is saying rotten things about another girl in front of the guys whenever she gets a chance, and always in a way that makes the guys crack up. Then she tells the horror-stricken girl something like,

"Oh, lighten up, I was just making a joke!"

Right.

Last spring, she was playing doubles tennis with Alyssa. They were beating this awesome doubles team from Lakewood, but when these gorgeous guys showed up and started scoping out Alyssa, who was playing on the half of the court closer to the stands, Margot served the ball low and hit Alyssa in the rear end, totally on purpose. While Alyssa was adjusting her tennis skirt and giving Margot a dirty look, Margot fired an ace for her next serve.

You'd think people would catch on, but the problem is that Margot looks like a Swedish supermodel, and she's into sports that show off her long legs—cheerleading in the fall, tennis in the spring. Of course, once the guys from Lakewood noticed her in her way-short tennis skirt—and saw Alyssa looking stupid, rubbing her rear where Margot nailed her—it was game over for Alyssa.

"It is true, though," Rachel says over her shoulder to Amy. "The most hated girls in school are some of the prettiest ones—"

"No," I interrupt, not wanting to discuss this anymore. "Heinous, evil, manipulative rat bitches are the ones who are hated. Otherwise, you two would be hated too, and you're not. I mean, you're both pretty decent looking yourselves. Plus, Amy, you're a superathlete and Rachel's got the best fashion sense of anyone I know."

They look at each other and shrug. They know Margot's awful, even if she is one of those cheerleaders who impresses people because she can actually do the back handsprings and all that flippy stuff, but I guess they'd rather make their point—whatever it is—than admit that they're wrong. "Whatever," Rachel says. "It's not like it matters."

Amy gives me a lopsided grin. "Yeah, we just wanted you to feel better. You know, with Sean so far away and everything."

They start talking about this gorgeous new guy Rachel heard transferred in from Fort Collins, and as we walk toward honors English I tell myself that it really is nothing, that they were just killing time before assembly with all their pretty-girl yakking, then tune them out. I mean, we all know how we're labeled. We've talked about it several times over the last few years. We've decided that everyone in school considers Rachel the fashion plate, Amy the jock, and our friend Kendra the brainiac. Of course, I'm the pretty one with a boyfriend. (Kendra always adds the "with a boyfriend" part, probably because she's never really had one and therefore finds this an important distinction.)

But whenever we talk about it, we say it sarcastically and talk about how it doesn't mean anything 'cause it's all surface stuff, and in any school the size of Vista Verde High (huge), you're bound to get labeled. The way most people use the labels in conversation, they're nothing more than a handy reference tool—like saying, 'the goth from biology' or 'the granola girl from volleyball' just so everyone knows who you're talking about. It's not necessarily a be-all, end-all character judgment. So I'm just going to go right on assuming that Rachel and Amy consider the pretty thing surface stuff.

All I can think about is Sean, anyway. How we won't be eating lunch together today. How he won't be waiting for me after school. How he's never, ever going to kiss me again or hold my hand during football games or the movies or tell me I'm scary beautiful.

I'm just wondering how I can break the news to Amy and Rachel and my other friends. And if they really can get past the "with a boyfriend" label I've had for so long.

As it turns out, Amy breaks the news to me, thanks to the rumor mill. Sean must've e-mailed some people here once he got to Connecticut to give them his new e-mail addy. From what Amy can figure out, he used the opportunity to drop the breakup bomb, and it got back to her before it got back to me.

Figures.

"What is *with* you? How come you didn't say anything?" She's practically screaming into the phone, so I hold my cell a few inches from my ear while I push my trig homework aside. Thank goodness it's almost done, because I know this conversation is gonna take a while. And it's not like I understand quadratic functions that well anyway. (Do they really have a purpose?)

"I sounded like a total idiot," she continues, "telling Eric Biedermeyer that he was lying out his ass, and that you and Sean are totally together, so whoever told him you weren't was full of it. But Eric wasn't lying to me, was he? Why didn't you say something?"

She's quiet for half a breath, then says, "Is it because of what I said at the assembly this morning?"

"Amy—"

"No, couldn't have been," she answers her own question. "Sean left a couple days before school even started. And you could've said something at the lockers if you'd wanted to tell me—"

"I wanted to, really, but I wasn't ready." Though, truth be told, their pretty-girl discussion didn't help matters. "I just couldn't deal yet, especially on the first day of school."

"Well . . . what a shitkicker, Chloe."

I can't help laughing. That's always Amy's word: "shit." She uses it in more forms than anyone I've ever met. Then again, she's the total potty mouth among us, whereas I almost never swear (and feel

26

horribly guilty when I do . . . I even have a hard time letting loose with "ass" instead of "butt" or "rear end"), so maybe I'm just more sensitive to her penchant for it.

I hear her exhale, then her whole tone changes. "I'm so sorry. I know you must feel awful. I shouldn't have gotten mad at you for not telling me, either. Forgive me for being so nasty? I can hang up and call back. Start the whole phone call over—"

"It's okay." I interrupt, relaxing a bit now that she's overapologizing. I mean, I really should have told her the minute I got home from the airport. I know if something like that had happened to her, she'd have called me from her cell phone *in* the airport. "And I'm sorry you found out from Eric Biedermeyer. You know you would've been the first person I told once I worked up the guts."

"I know." I can picture her walking around her bedroom, maybe even grabbing one of the dumbbells from where they sit near her radiator so she can work her biceps while she talks. It's her way of slowing down and trying to focus. "I—I guess I'm just surprised. I figured you guys would be together forever. Like you'd be able to see each other on breaks and then go to college together and everything would work out. If anyone could do the long-distance thing for two years, I figured it'd be you guys."

She's not the only one. Dumb, dumb, dumb me.

"And I didn't mean what I said at assembly, about everyone hating you. I was just shooting off at the mouth trying to convince you that you looked good, so you wouldn't be mopey all day, you know? And I'm positive Rachel meant it the same way."

"I know." Sort of. "Thanks."

"So . . . um, how'd it happen?"

The million-dollar question. I close my eyes for a moment, trying to think of how to say this so Amy will understand that I don't exactly want the details spread around the school, but without making it sound like I think she'd do that. As I'm about to speak, a pinging sound comes from my computer.

"Hold on. Someone's IMing me." I untangle myself from my homework and cross the room to my desk. "Oh, man. Get this. It's Margot deVries."

"Ooooooh. Read it! Read it!"

Margot32: R U there? Heard Sean dumped U at DIA. Totally rude! Wanted 2 let U know I'm thinking of U. R U OK?

"It says she heard about Sean and is thinking of me," I tell Amy, verbally editing Margot's IM. I cannot freaking believe Sean is telling people we broke up at the airport. I wonder if I should ask Margot where she heard—just so I'd know who's talking to whom here—but decide against it.

"Yeah, she's thinking of you, all right," Amy snorts. "And how it pisses her off that Sean's across the country so she can't make a move."

I laugh at this because it's probably true.

"So you gonna answer her?"

"Nah. My idle message is on, so she'll think I'm not here." I hate to be impolite. I guess it's just gut instinct for me to respond when someone sends me an instant message. But I think, for now, and especially with Margot, it's better to lie low.

"Smart girl," Amy says. "Hey, does Rachel know yet?"

"Not from me. I haven't told anyone."

"Well, she'd better hear it from you before she hears it from someone else. Like Margot."

"Agreed."

"It's only five thirty, and I haven't eaten yet," Amy says. "Wanna meet at WooWoo's? We can get away from most of the Vista Verde types there, plus the place always puts Rachel in a good mood."

"Sure. I can pick you up in about twenty minutes." Dad's working late tonight, so I'm on my own for dinner. He won't mind as long as I leave a note letting him know where I am. And WooWoo Pizza, this psychedelic pizza spot that's a few miles away in Boulder, is my absolute fave place to eat. "I'll call Rachel."

"Kendra, too?"

"Kendra, too." It's bad enough that I hardly got to see her at school today, let alone as much as I should have all summer long. She'll be ticked off—and rightfully so—if she hears the Sean news through the grapevine.

"Twenty minutes," Amy says, then hangs up.

TWO

"He knew for three days he was going to break up with you?"

Kendra's mouth is hanging open, and I'm tempted to reach across the slick red table and gently push it shut. But since she's usually the most levelheaded of our little group—totally a straight-A student and the most Zen-like of the four of us—I figure I should cut her some slack.

"Yeah," I say as casually as possible. I appreciate their support, but don't want this to turn into a total pity party, either. "I guess ever since we did the MapQuest thing. He just waited till the airport to tell me."

"What a chickenshit," Amy says as she plays with the big plastic number 5 that tells the WooWoo Pizza employees which table needs which pie. "I mean, you know I've always liked Sean, but that was beyond lame. It's probably the first-ever MapQuest breakup on record."

"I kind of understand it, though." Rachel shrugs, giving Amy a sheepish look. "They were together a long time. You can't just see some driving directions on a piece of paper, have this lightning moment, and then pop out with, 'Yo, that's it, baby! I'm outta here!' He probably had to think about what he wanted to say."

"And dumping her at DIA was better?" Amy snaps back. Amy always claims to be as calm as Kendra, but really, she has a temper. Quick to anger—but quick to chill, so I know she'll get over being angry with Sean pretty fast.

"I think he just hadn't figured out what to say, and time had run out. So he had to say something before he got on the plane," Rachel says, fumbling to rationalize Sean's behavior. She looks at me. "Not that I want to make excuses for him, Chloe. What he did was horrible. But I know he's really a great guy."

"I haven't told you guys the best part," I reply. I wad up the wrapper from my straw, then roll it around the table with my thumb. "We were sitting in Pour la France when he did it. Joe and Darcy got up to run to the restroom and left Sean and me to watch their carry-on bags. So we had, like, two minutes alone. That's when he did it. And he was clearly planning to do it then, because I saw him give Joe this look first, and that's when Joe said he needed to use the restroom and Darcy instantly jumped up to go too."

"They all three planned it? So it wasn't just a last-minute thing where he couldn't put it off anymore?" Rachel sounds stunned, as she should. I mean, I'm still in complete shock myself. Well, maybe past being shocked and into being ticked off at him.

"Nope," I say. "At least, it didn't feel that way. But the worst part is that I didn't even get to say anything about it. Right after Sean dropped his bomb, the waiter came up with the check and insisted on standing there and asking us if we'd like to fill out a customer satisfaction survey. By the time we got rid of him, Joe and Darcy were back."

"And you didn't get a chance to talk to Sean alone after that?" Kendra asks, back to her analytical self.

"Nope. Darcy paid the bill and said they should hurry to their gate because it was clear out at the end of Concourse B, and they had to get through security and take the underground train thingie to get out there, yadda yadda, hurry hurry, blah blah blah." I make a flippy motion with my hand, and they all nod their understanding. They've met Darcy, so they know she's one of those people who's super-cautious and preplans everything.

Maybe including the military precision of her brother's breakup.

"He did call me on his cell from Chicago, since they had a layover there," I add. "I think he felt guilty. I told him it was okay and that I understood. The call lasted all of thirty seconds. I mean, what could I say at that point?"

"You should have just told him to blow

it out—," Amy starts, but Kendra interrupts by saying, "What good would that do? And what could Sean have said from Chicago, anyway, since Darcy and Joe were probably standing right there?"

"Probably not much that he would have said without them there," I tell them. "He hasn't bothered to call back or e-mail me since. If he wanted to, he could have called me anytime after he got to Connecticut."

Kendra looks back to me and says, "Who would have thought, after you were together so long? And you were so perfect! I'm so sorry, Chloe."

Rachel's nodding, but only half paying attention, because WooWoo Pizza Guy is heading toward our table. Rachel's had a mild crush on him since the beginning of the summer, when he started working here, and I can see why. She doesn't know his name, but we know from a comment we overheard once at the pizza counter that he's a senior and he's planning to go to Colorado State next year. We think he must go to a different high school, 'cause none of us recall having seen him around ours (which is good, because this way, he doesn't know any of our dirt other than what he might have overheard us talking about in WooWoo.) He's hot in a doesn't-care-about-his-looks kind of way. He has sun-bleached, wavy blond hair and he strikes me as brainy but still kind of athletic, which is right up Rachel's alley.

Of course, half the guys in our high school are right up Rachel's alley. She's a first-class flirt and has a new crush every week. If we weren't here for the sole purpose of discussing my breakup with Sean, I'm sure we'd all be hearing whatever she found out about the cute new guy who transferred in from Fort Collins. Whenever Rachel's not busy reeling in guys, she's talking about them.

"Order number five? Cheese and mushrooms?" he asks as he sets it on the table, even though by now he probably knows that's what we order every time we come. He scans the table, picks up the plastic claim number, then focuses on Rachel's empty cup. "Can I get you another drink? You had Diet Pepsi, right?"

"That'd be great, thanks." She hands him her red plastic cup, and I notice that her fingers brush against his when he takes it.

When his back is turned, we all grin at one another.

"Woo woo," Amy mouths, which totally cracks me up.

After we all take a slice and are settled with napkins, I tell them thanks, just for listening and understanding.

"Hey, we do," Kendra says, and I know she means it. "And I'm glad you asked us out to WooWoo to give us the dirty details, even though I know you weren't really ready to talk about it yet."

Amy takes a bite of pizza and, with her mouth full, says, "Freakin' Eric Biedermeyer. I never would've thought he'd be a gossip. Theoretically, Sean was his friend."

"No," I say. "Freakin' Sean Norcross." Because, really, any gossip is his fault. He should have let me tell everyone. He knows me well enough to know that I wouldn't have wanted the breakup broadcast around school until I was ready.

"Well, I don't think that many people knew about it at school today," Kendra says, and Rachel and Amy both murmur their agreement. "I hadn't heard until Amy called."

"And really, I think Eric only asked me because I'm your friend," Amy says.

"Good. I don't want to be the focus of gossip."

They all look at each other. "I don't think you can avoid it now," Rachel finally says, and I know she's thinking about my IM from Margot deVries, which Amy naturally brought up the minute I confirmed to everyone that, yes, there had been a breakup and yes, at least Eric Biedermeyer knew about it already. "By tomorrow, it'll be all over school. But we'll do our best to make it sound like you're cool with it, okay?"

"Thanks."

WooWoo Pizza Guy returns with Rachel's drink, and I know we all must look totally pathetic smiling at him. There's just something about him that transcends the tie-dyed WooWoo Pizza apron they make him wear.

"Everything all right here?" he asks, and we all nod like idiots.

"Great."

He's about to leave, when Rachel pops out with, "One suggestion, though. You guys really need to wear name tags."

He pauses, then hooks his thumbs in the wraparound ties of his WooWoo apron. "Why's that?"

"So I know what to call you, of course."

He gives Rachel a totally obvious once-over. "You're not wearing a name tag."

"I'm the customer. And it's Rachel."

"I know. I'm Billy," he says, and then Rachel introduces all of us. Even though he's smiling, it's a little off-kilter, like he finds all of this odd. When Rachel's done, he says, "I have to get back to the counter, but just call me if you need anything."

Once he's gone, Rachel says, "Oh, I'd like to call him, all right. Even if his name is *Billy*. Has anyone named their kid Bill or Billy in the last, oh, twenty years?"

Amy tells her that she should call him, or at least flirt with him at the counter a little and maybe find a way to slip him her phone number or e-mail addy. If he'd been paying enough attention to our conversations over the summer that he knew Rachel's name, he was probably at least a little interested.

Then Amy looks at me and says, "You,

too. Not with Billy, I mean, but someone. Get out and flirt a little. Even if you're not looking for a boyfriend or anything right now, I bet it makes you feel better."

It would so *not*. Kendra—a total non-flirt, like me—gets it, because she shoots me a look like, *Is she for real?* But since Amy and Rachel (especially Rachel) are the types who feel comfortable doing that kind of thing, I don't say anything.

"Just make sure it's someone Margot's after," Rachel teases. "I can't believe her IM to you. Totally transparent."

"Let's not talk about Margot. You'd be better off to steer clear of her and her entire crowd." Kendra can't even say Margot's name without disgust in her voice, especially after they got into it last winter when Margot made a nasty comment about Kendra to this guy Kendra'd been crushing on, just because Margot wanted some attention. It was one of those backhanded compliments, something like, "Oh, Kendra's hair's just frizzy because she doesn't take the time to style it, you know, with all the hard-core studying she does. She's such an egghead. . . ." It was said in a way that made Kendra sound like she was lucky she hadn't contracted some foul disease from studying so hard.

"No problem there," I say. I really don't know Margot that well, but I did witness the incident with Alyssa and have heard enough other stories—like Kendra's—to have a good fix on her type. "No way do I want to be on Margot's radar screen."

My cell phone rings, and it's Dad asking me if I can swing by the grocery store on the way home to grab some popcorn. We always watch TV together on Monday nights, so I know this is also his way of checking up on me to see if I'll make it home in time for our usual sitcoms.

I finish up my slice, drop some money on the table, and tell the girls I have to get home. Rachel says she can give both Amy and Kendra a ride, so we're cool.

Since it's just me and Dad, they never complain when I ditch early to hang out with him. Besides, I figure they'll want the time to talk about me after I leave, and try to decide whether I'm really okay.

I hope I've convinced them—even if I haven't convinced myself.

• • •

"So," Dad says during the second commercial break, "I guess you're going to mope for a couple weeks? Or should I count on a full month?"

I take a long sip of my Diet Coke, refusing to look at him. "Very funny."

"Apparently not. You haven't cracked a smile yet, and this is one of the best episodes we've seen. Or did you mean my crack about you moping when you said, 'Very funny'? I've always thought I'm a funny guy, but you know—"

I flick a piece of popcorn toward his nose but miss and hit the cat, who snarls at me.

Dad picks up the popcorn, which ended up on the floor in front of the sofa where he's sitting, then pops it in his mouth.

"That's gross, Dad." I don't know why I bother telling him anymore. I mean, you'd think I'd be used to living with no other women in the house, since I've never really known anything else. My mom died in a car accident when I was five and I only have vague memories of her. Specific incidents, mostly, like sitting in her favorite chair with her to pick an Easter dress out of a catalog, or watching her fall down in the snow and laughing about it, even though we were on our way to church and she got so soaking wet that we ended up not going. But I can't remember whether she was more strict with me than Dad is, or how she kept the house or anything like that. Or even if she'd have been the kind of mother I could talk to about what really happened with Sean.

He kicks back so his feet are on the coffee table and looks to where I'm sprawled on the love seat with my popcorn bowl balanced on my stomach. "I take it the first day of school was tough?"

"School was fine."

"I meant because of Sean. How'd you do?"

I know he's trying to be friendly, subtly letting me know he won't butt in but I can talk to him if I need to. And usually, I do talk to him about stuff. We're really tight, probably because he treats me more like an adult than most parents treat their kids. It's partially out of necessity, since I'm the one who does most of the grocery shopping, runs to the post office, and handles all the other errands most of my friends' moms do, and partially because I think he prefers talking to me on an adult level. But in this instance, I have to remember that he's still my dad and, well, a *guy*. More specifically, a sure-to-be-bald-someday, single guy who's a couple years past forty.

"Chloe?"

"Dad, I'm here, right? So clearly I survived."

He pauses to watch a commercial for some mutual fund company—since he works for a mutual fund company in Denver, he always perks up with he sees ads for the competition—then asks, "Do you have plans this weekend?"

"Not yet. The Andersons said they might need a sitter for a while Saturday afternoon, but otherwise I figured I'd just go to the movies with Amy or something. Why?"

"Nothing specific. Just wanted to make sure you're getting out and doing things. You've spent a lot of your free time on the weekends with Sean the last two years."

"But usually in a group. Really, Dad, I'm fine." And Charlie Sheen is back on TV now, so I really want to pay attention. Charlie might be getting old, but he's still decent looking and entirely too witty for his own good.

As we watch Charlie hit on a gorgeous, long-legged brunette with a supermodel body, it occurs to me that I'm lucky Dad's the way he is. If anyone asked me, I'd have to admit that Dad's still good looking enough to go out and pick up pretty much whomever he wants. But instead, he only goes out on dates once in a while, keeps 'em all fairly casual, and mostly spends his time focused on work and on me. (Well, and occasionally on duck hunting, which I find repugnant but he claims is just another "networking opportunity" since he goes with all these other financial types.) It also occurs to me as Charlie Sheen fails to snag the girl (again) that maybe Charlie's got a good attitude about experiencing life. He doesn't get too down about anything. He cracks a few jokes and then goes right on looking for the next opportunity.

Not that I'm looking to move on to another boyfriend, especially since I'm still (stupidly, deep down inside) hoping that Sean will wake up one morning soon, call me, and say it was a huge, moment-of-panic mistake and that he loves me more than anything. That he can't wait to come see me at Christmas, and maybe he can manage to get out here sooner if he's careful with his money.

But since the odds of that happening are clearly zero, I decide as I watch the show that I need to develop that Charlie Sheen attitude in myself. The whole losing-a-hot-girl-is-no-big-deal thing isn't just an act with him. He's truly optimistic that another gorgeous girl is just around the corner, waiting to meet him, and that maybe she'll be The One.

He makes being single look cool and fun. Not lonely at all.

Come to think of it, so does Dad.

When the show's over, I wash out my popcorn bowl, talk with Dad a little about maybe going to a Nuggets game in a few weeks if he can get tickets, then excuse myself so I can finish my homework. But before I go to bed, I e-mail Amy, explain my Charlie Sheen revelation, and then tell her that I'm determined to be a Cool Single Person, to not let the whole Sean thing get to me, and that if I stray from the path, I want her to call me on it.

She IMs me back within a minute to tell me it's a done deal.

She probably sees it as a challenge, and, being her competitive self, she's never backed down from a challenge.

"Okay, I don't know what I was thinking," I tell Amy two days later. "I'm not Charlie Sheen. I can't just put him out of my head."

We're walking from our lockers to honors English, and all I can think about is how Sean should be in honors English too. How I read the assignment all alone in my room last night instead of over at Sean's, curled up on his bed while he lounged in his beanbag chair, reading right along beside me.

"Huh?" Amy sidesteps a group of senior jocks who are hogging the hallway, then frowns at me. "You can't put Charlie Sheen out of your head?"

"No, no. I mean Sean. Remember how I told you on Monday night that I need to adopt a Charlie Sheen attitude? That I need to put myself in the mindset that I should enjoy being single, because there's absolutely nothing wrong with it?"

Amy shoots me a total death look.

"Come on, you know I'm not slamming singledom," I backtrack. "I've always thought that you're a Cool Single Person."

"Oh, I know I'm cool, but being single has nothing to do with my level of utter coolness," she says, casually hooking her thumb in her front jeans pocket as if to prove that she is, well, cool. "And it's not like I don't want a boyfriend, 'cause believe me, I know exactly what I'd do with one if—"

"I know, I know." I hold up a hand to prevent her from giving me the details. "But follow along here. I'm saying that I think you have the Charlie attitude. You're not with anyone, even though you'd like to be. And if it doesn't happen right away, then it's no big thing to you. You're happy being you. All I'm saying is that I'm trying to be that way, but it's not working because I can't put Sean out of my head."

"Oh, that's right. I'm supposed to be reminding you to forget about Sean."

So much for my thinking she was taking this as a challenge.

"Were you thinking about him just now?" she asks.

"Of course."

She reaches out and whomps me on the forehead. Not real hard (especially for her), but with enough force to make me yelp.

"Is my duty done?" she asks as a couple of sophomores I recognize from tennis pass us, giggling. "Is he out of your head?"

"Um, no." I put a hand to my forehead and glare at her. This wasn't what I meant by calling me on it if I didn't develop a Cool Single Person attitude. "Seriously, Amy, how do you do it?"

I know I sound like a moron asking her this, but it's slowly dawning on me that I've been living in a bubble since the second half of eighth grade, which is a really long time. Yeah, I'm pretty tight with Amy, Rachel, and Kendra, and it's not like I've ignored them and totally focused on Sean, like a lot of girls do when they get a boyfriend. But now I'm realizing that half my life revolved around him and half around my friends. Now with one half gone, I'm totally off-balance. How'd I ever allow myself to get this way?

"I just do it, I guess," Amy says with a shrug. "Look, you're going to feel yucky for a while. I don't think there's anything you can do about it but give it time."

We settle into our desk chairs, and I take a deep breath. I need to focus on *Beowulf*, not on Sean. If I don't, I'm going to drive myself—and Amy—nuts, plus I need to get a good grade in this class so I can get into AP English next year.

Amy leans across the aisle. "Hey, maybe you can try out for a fall sport. I know you've never been much of a joiner, other than tennis in the spring, but you're in good shape. You run. What about cross-country? It'll give you something to do."

"Are you serious?"

She nods. "Yeah, the more I think about it, it'd be perfect. You could meet some new people, get out of your rut. And running is the best way I know to clear your brain. Works for me, anyway."

"That's because you're you, Amy. I run the absolute bare minimum required to keep myself ready for tennis season." Well, and to keep from feeling like a slug after too many nights in a row of takeout with Dad.

"No one says you have to break records.

Do it for fun. You're good enough to make the team, whether you think you are or not. And I know they're looking. Tryouts actually started last week, before school started, but they didn't get as many people as they wanted, so it's still open."

I have to admit, Amy's idea is pretty good. It would get me out of the house during the hours right after school, which is when I used to spend time with Sean. But I wouldn't want to try out and then be the suckiest member of the team either. I frown at Amy. "I bet no one goes out for the first time as a junior. I mean, other juniors have all been doing this—"

"So what?" Amy silences me with a glare. She has a way of doing it that's even more powerful than a whack to the forehead. "Either go out or don't go out. You asked for my help, and so I'm helping. And it's not like it's forever. You can always quit if you decide you don't like it. What's it hurt to try?"

The last bell rings, and everyone who's been standing around talking flops into their seats. Mr. Whiddicomb was sitting at his desk in the back of the room writing when Amy and I came in, but the second the bell finishes reverberating, he's like a rocket getting to the front so he can get started. A few of the geek types in the first row already have their books out and pencils and paper ready to take notes.

Some people are entirely too into *Beowulf.*

"What time's practice start?" I whisper to Amy.

"Quarter to three."

Problem. I gesture toward my sandal-clad feet. I won't have enough time to get home and back.

"Borrow mine."

Right. The girl's a solid size ten, and I'm a nine, sometimes a half size smaller, depending on the brand. Mr. Whiddicomb starts up about *Beowulf,* talking about symbolism, so I can't say anything. But a minute later, a note comes sliding across the aisle from Amy.

Just stuff cotton or something in the toes. They're not gonna run you hard your first day. I have clean socks and whatever other clothes you might need in my gym locker. DO IT!!!

Since she has softball after school and usually brings all her softball clothes for the week on Mondays, I figure her locker's pretty well stocked. And she's right: I either need to put up or shut up. I glance her way and mouth, "Okay."

Though I'm thinking Charlie Sheen never had to run cross-country in oversize shoes to shake things up.

As it turns out, the big shake-up ends up happening in fifth period, when I have independent study. I'm supposed to be working out a curriculum for myself, explaining what I'll learn in my self-taught history of the Middle East, but all I can do is gawk at the guy sitting under the windows on the other side of the computer lab.

Under my desk I pull out my cell phone as subtly as possible and text-message Amy. I'm not sure if she'll have hers on—and, I hope, silenced—but this is too important to not tell her immediately.

Within two minutes, a message from Amy pops up on the screen of my cell phone.

NO WAY. U SURE?

Oh, I'm sure. I look at the guy sitting near the windows again. He has his back to me, but when he turns to the side to flip through his notebook, I get a good look.

WEARING GLASSES, BUT DEF. WOOWOO.

He goes to our school after all. And he must be doing independent study too, since there's no class in here this period. He hasn't been in here before, but he could have been working in the library or meeting with whichever teacher is sponsoring him on the first two days of classes.

Amy text messages back. I don't know how she's doing this in chemistry class. Ms. Cooper might have an easier curve than some teachers, but she's a hard-ass about people using cell phones in class.

DOES RACHEL KNOW?

The computer lab monitor gets up from her desk to make a lap through the room and check on everyone—probably to make sure we're not downloading porn—so I quickly pocket the phone. I focus on my computer screen and type something generic about why I think it's important for those of us living in the United States to understand the Middle East from a historical perspective.

Once the lab monitor is back behind her desk, satisfied that no one is playing fantasy football online or otherwise goofing off, I slide my cell phone out of my pocket and type a message back to Amy.

NOT YET.

The more I study WooWoo (discreetly, of course), the more I realize why we—well, why Rachel in particular—never noticed him before. Aside from the fact that our school has over two thousand students and he's a senior and we're juniors, I mean.

He's kind of a geek. Okay, more than kind of. He *is* a geek. A full-throttle, out-and-out geek.

He has a very techie-looking calculator on the desk beside him, and from what I can see of his notebook, he has lots of graphs and formulas scribbled in there. They don't look like they were neatly copied from some textbook. There are arrows and scribbles all over the place, like this is something he came up with on his own. He doesn't look like he's stressed working on it either.

In fact, he looks like he's enjoying it. Like he's some kind of mad genius.

You don't exactly notice that geek factor when he's wearing a tie-dyed WooWoo uniform and doling out pizzas and Diet Pepsi. I've always gotten the impression he has a brain, but I hadn't quite pictured this.

Then it hits me. No wonder he gave us funny looks when Rachel introduced herself. It wasn't just that he'd overheard her name at the pizza place; he knew our names from school.

Rachel will die of embarrassment if she figures it out.

He signs off his computer, stuffs his books in his backpack, then walks up to the lab monitor and says something. A minute later, she hands him a hall pass—presumably to the library, since that's where we're supposed to be for independent study if we're not in the computer lab—and warns him to go straight there and not to linger in the hallways.

As if someone who looks like he does is going to take the opportunity to ditch. Right.

As he walks out he looks my way and catches me staring. Then he smiles, because he knows I recognize him. Behind the glasses, I can see he's still cute WooWoo. The messy blond hair, the hint of mischief in his blue eyes. The fact that he's a bit of a loner, taking an independent study class that's clearly heavy on the math and science while most seniors are indulging in post-lunch snoozefests in AP English or whatever difficult-sounding-but-really-a-breeze class they think will look good on their transcript.

And in that split second, I know that things have changed between him and my whole group of friends. I'm not sure how, but they have. Like he's more than just the WooWoo Pizza Guy. And I'm more than just the pretty girl with her loudmouthed, gossipy, athletic/fashionable/brainiac friends who stake out the corner booth.

"See ya, Chloe," he says.

"See ya, Billy," I tell him. And I smile back.

Three

I think I'm going to hurl. I picture Amy's scribbled note, assuring me that the cross-country coach won't run me hard the first day, and all I can think is, *Yeah, right.*

If I ever get the strength, I'm going to strangle her.

It doesn't help matters that Eric Biedermeyer is running all of three feet off my left elbow with a loopy, adrenaline-induced grin on his face. "You okay, Chloe?"

"Fine," I grunt out, trying to focus on where my feet are going. "Ate too much at lunch, I think."

I would give anything to be sitting in my bedroom right now, e-mailing back and forth with Kendra or trying to find an online picture of whatever hot guy Rachel saw in *Teen People* and is raving about so I can tell her if I agree. But I'm determined to make it through at least one practice with my dignity intact, even if it means running harder than I should, given that I'm wearing too-big shoes and that I've engaged in virtually zero physical activity all summer. Well, other than physical activity of the sort I engaged in with Sean, but I refuse to let my brain go there.

"Run much over the summer?" Eric asks.

"Sure. Marathons." Jerk. He knows exactly what I did over the summer, and whom I was doing it with. The two of them have hung out together for years.

"Look, I'm not trying to be rude," he says as we round a curve in the trail and I nearly trip over some scrubby brush that's sticking out into the path. "Just making conversation. Wondering how you're doing."

"I'm fine. Really." If fine constitutes being closer to the end of the course than I was when he started talking to me.

We run along in silence for a while, pounding out step after step on the hard trail through the evergreens. I can't figure out why he doesn't just run on ahead. There are a lot of us running the course, mostly in packs, but some in ones and twos. If he sped up just a little, he could catch a friend of his I saw turn the corner ahead of us.

He could run with anyone but me.

"Just about everyone has it rough in the beginning, you know."

I mumble something back, intentionally sounding grumbly so he'll stop. I really don't want to have a conversation. There's still a mile or so to go, and I need the energy. I figured the coach would have us stretch a lot and maybe talk for part of the practice—not that he'd have us run three miles right off the bat—so I'm not sure I was mentally ready to do this.

I don't remember the last time I ran three miles. I'm a tennis player. I run in bursts. And even when I run for exercise—which is rare—I go a mile, maybe two, and then do some stretching or power yoga. It makes me feel better afterward—all gooey and loose and relaxed physically and laser-sharp mentally. I'm not sure this will improve my mental state one iota, despite what Amy promised me as I laced her Nikes onto my feet, complete with a wad of toilet paper in each toe, and tried not to ask her again why this would get me out of my funk.

So since hitting the course, I've been trying to focus on what else I need to put in my history of the Middle East syllabus, just to distract myself. I even daydreamed about WooWoo Pizza Guy for a good half mile before I realized that I was being Charlie Sheen-esque in a bad way. As in, mentally scamming on a guy Rachel's already got on her radar, even if he is an über-geek.

Still . . . anything to keep from thinking about Sean. Or about the nasty runner's ick creeping up in my stomach at the same time a trickle of sweat is running front and center down my borrowed sports bra.

I can tell Eric's about to say something else, so I muster up enough breath to speak politely. "You don't have to worry about me, Eric. I promise not to collapse and die of exhaustion or anything."

He laughs at this. "I wasn't worried about that. I was more worried about you just in general."

Great. "You mean because of Sean?"

"Yeah."

"Oh. Well, again, I'm fine." Mentally I add a *please don't make me talk anymore*.

Two senior girls pass us on the right. I know Eric could run way faster if he wanted to. One of the girls looks back over her shoulder at Eric, trying to check him out without being too obvious about it. I glance over at him and see that he noticed her noticing him. He's even blushing. I don't think the red in his cheeks is from the run, because he can't be running that hard if he's running with me.

"You can go faster if you want," I tell him. "I don't mind." Especially if he's running with me to talk about Sean. I'm here to get away from thinking about Sean.

"No, it's no problem," he says in a voice that makes me think he has zero interest in either of the two seniors. "We're going plenty fast, especially for practice." He runs his hand over his hair, as if he's all sweaty, but I don't see an ounce of moisture up there.

It's disgusting what good shape Eric's in. Just like Sean.

Argh! Stop it, brain, Stop it, stop it.

"I actually wanted to run with you when I saw you show up to practice," he says. "I wanted to tell you that I'm sorry about yesterday. I didn't mean to blab to Amy about the breakup and all."

I give him a look like, *So why did you?*

He shrugs. "I assumed that you'd told your friends already. Margot deVries was acting all worried about you."

"Really? I don't know her that well." Just well enough to know Margot brought up my oh-so-fragile emotional health for her own reasons. The bigger question, though, was how the hell Margot deVries knew about the breakup if Eric wasn't the one who told her? Had she heard from some other friend of Sean's?

Or—perish the thought—from Sean himself? No, he wouldn't e-mail her with the news. Why would he?

"Yeah, she stopped by my table at lunch yesterday and asked if I knew how you were doing." He takes a stutter step to avoid a rock in the path, then says, "Since

Margot knew about you and Sean, I figured everyone knew. And I asked Amy how you were doing because I thought coming to you directly would be awkward. You know, since I used to hang out with Sean. I didn't want you to think I was butting into your business or spying on you for him or anything."

"Were you?"

"No. Think I'd be talking to you about it right now if I were? I just wanted to make sure you were okay. And I wanted to tell Amy that even though you and Sean broke up, it's still cool with me if you two want to hang out every so often. Just 'cause Sean's not around anymore, you know, doesn't mean . . ."

"Well, thanks. I appreciate that." I point out a huge tree we run by—anything to change the subject—and tell him I wonder how many runners over the years have hidden behind it to pee.

He laughs, saying he saw a guy from Arvada do it once during a meet. But as we near the school again—Hallelujah! Relief! I can rest!—he asks me if Amy's mad at him.

"Um, I don't think so. She was just surprised, is all." I'm the one she was mad at—at least temporarily.

We leave the path and the evergreens behind, emerging at a fence that borders the high school baseball fields. The girls' softball team is out there now, and Eric looks past me, toward where Amy's standing at shortstop. She has her back to us, waiting for the girl at bat to whack the softball her direction.

"Well, I guess that's good," he says, tipping his head in Amy's direction. "I mean, I wouldn't want to piss her off or anything."

No, no one wants to piss off Amy. I'm about to crack a joke when I hear, "Eric! Hustle up! You're behind today!" The cross-country coach is standing at the edge of the track, just past the baseball fields, holding a stopwatch in his hand. To make an even 3.1 mile run, everyone coming off the cross-country trail has to do one lap around the track. I get the impression he's going to yell out the times as everyone crosses the finish line.

I hope I make it without yakking

everywhere. Or having anyone laugh when they hear my time.

"Chloe! Good job! Keep it up!"

Good job for me, but hustle up to Eric? Eric obviously reads my thoughts because he mutters, "Totally unfair."

"Go," I tell him.

"Yeah, I'd better." He kicks it and gets ahead of me pretty fast. Before I know it, he's done with his lap, and I'm only halfway around the track.

Thank God I'm not the last one, though. I still see some girls coming out of the trees, just making it to the place where the trail ends and the bumpy area behind the baseball field fence begins.

Actually, as I turn onto the last stretch of track and get a good view back the way I came, I realize that I'm far from last. The two senior girls who passed us are done, and there are four or five guys with their hands on their hips, walking around on the inside of the track trying to catch their breath.

Then there's Eric. Then me. Everyone else is still running.

"Great effort, Chloe," Coach McCarthy

says as I cross the line. I try not to breathe too hard, but I am so about to die.

If I'd been paying attention for the first mile or two—instead of daydreaming about Sean and WooWoo Pizza Guy Billy—I might've realized that I wasn't behind everyone else. I could have slowed down.

"Thanks," I manage.

"Have you been running this summer?"

I want to lie and say I have, but I just blurt out, "Um, not really."

"Well, you clocked in at 21:08."

I know it sounds stupid, but I ask, "Is that good?"

His face splits into a wide grin. "For a five-kilometer course? Knock a little off that, and you'll be earning us some serious points in meets."

He doesn't look like he's feeding me a line of bull, so I just mumble an okay, then head toward the grass to grab my water bottle while he yells toward a pack of guys just now getting to the track.

Maybe I can do this after all, if I keep practicing. Well, once my lungs stop feeling like they're on fire.

I rummage through my backpack, find the bottle of water I bought from the machine in the locker room, then chug down half. It'll probably make my stomach worse, but I don't care.

I watch as the last of the runners emerge from the trees, then I glance down into my backpack at my cell phone. It says I missed two calls, so I discreetly dial my voice mail (since I don't know if this is a no-no where Coach McCarthy is concerned) and listen. One's from Dad, asking me to grab a pizza on the way home unless I'm in the mood to cook dinner (um, that's a negative), and the other's from Rachel. She heard about Billy from Amy and wants all the dirt.

I stuff the phone back in my backpack as everyone finishes up the run and the coach calls us all over to the area around the finish line to talk about future practices, what he expects from the team, and all that kind of thing. Despite being winded, everyone seems happy to be here. Most of them are people I don't know that well, but they seem nice enough. No Margot types at all. As I glance at them one by one, trying to memorize faces, I start to think that Amy was right. I might be able to distract myself with this—new friends, a physical challenge, the whole shebang. And it probably won't hurt my college applications to add another sport, either.

"Whatcha think, Chloe?" Eric asks after the coach finishes and we all start back toward the locker rooms.

"So far, so good," I say. He's grinning at me, and it's open and friendly. Not a sympathetic, I'm-sorry-my-friend-dumped-you-on-your-butt look at all, which is a relief. Most of Sean's friends seem to be ignoring me like the plague since the news broke.

"I'm glad you decided to try out," he says as we step from the track area onto the asphalt parking lot behind the gym, heading toward the locker rooms. "I wouldn't have picked you to be a runner, but I think you're gonna be really good."

Since Eric's pretty good himself, this is high praise. I feel like, for the first time, he's looking at me as someone separate from Sean. And I like that feeling.

"See you here tomorrow?" he says as he reaches for the door.

"Yeah." The word pops out without me thinking about it.

He smiles in return. "Good. And I meant what I said about you and Amy. If you wanna get together and hang out after practice sometime, that's cool. Let her know, okay?"

"Okay." Not sure I can picture us hanging out and being totally comfortable without Sean there, but as Eric turns into the guys' locker room, I decide that yes, I really meant what I told him about more cross-country. I just won't eat so much at lunch tomorrow.

I smile to myself as I cross the gym, headed for the girls' locker room. The softball team is coming in, so I stop at center court to wait for Amy so I can tell her how it all went. Before I can utter a single word, though, she grabs my elbow and pulls me a few steps back from the softball crowd. When the last girl enters the locker room and we're alone in the gym, she whispers, "What was that all about with Eric? I saw you running with him when you came in from the trail!"

"First he asked if I was okay post-Sean,

but then he wanted to know if you were pissed at him. You know, for spilling the beans," I explain. She's covered in red dirt, presumably from sliding into a base, and there's a dry, leathery odor coming from her glove. At least I assume it's her glove. Yeech. "I told him you weren't. He seemed kinda worried about it."

She looks surprised, but looks away to pick a clod of dirt out of her cleat. For a second, I think she's going to leave it on the gym floor, but she flicks it into one of the big gray trash barrels near the locker room door instead. "He should've been worried about it. He shouldn't be spreading rumors like that."

"It wasn't intentional. He thought you already knew. He felt bad about it, and he even said that if we wanted to hang out after practice sometime, that's cool with him, even though Sean and I aren't together anymore."

"Huh. Well, I still can't believe you kept up with him to talk about it. Good for you." She pulls off her baseball cap, then takes the elastic out of her hair to let down her ponytail. As we walk toward the locker room, she uses one hand to massage the back of her head, fluffing all the hair her hat smashed. She looks at me, wrinkling her nose. "Man, I reek. And you smell almost as bad as I do!"

I shake my head as we weave our way to the back of the locker room and find space on the bench in front of her locker. The place is crowded with softball players and cross-country types, all trying to get into their lockers or to the showers at the same time—and beat the cheerleaders, who'll be coming in any minute and will inevitably choke us all with their hair-spray.

"By the way, I didn't really keep up with Eric," I tell her. "He ran with me. I told him he could go ahead, but he didn't. Guess he really wanted to talk."

She shoots me a funny look as I take off her shoes and hand them back. I'm not sure if it's about Eric or about her shoes, which I have to admit are dirtier than when she gave them to me. I'm about to tell her about Eric's comment that he never wanted to piss her off, but before I can say any-thing, she shoves her cleats into her locker and tells me, "I'm not gonna shower here. I'll just do it at home. I've got a ton of trig to do tonight."

"Me too."

I know I should mention that I'm picking up pizza and can do a little spy work at WooWoo for Rachel on the way home, but Amy starts complaining about her Trig teacher, so I let it go.

"Half pepperoni, half cheese. Takeout," I tell the bored-looking girl behind the WooWoo counter. I can smell just the faintest odor of pot on her clothes, but maybe that's my imagination. There are lots of shakers with basil and oregano around the cooking area behind her.

I pay for the pizza, take the receipt with my pick-up number on it, then plop into a booth to wait. I knew I'd be stopping here, so I probably should have taken a shower, but when Amy skipped out and headed home, I left too.

I like showering at home better, anyway. I've never been totally comfortable getting naked in front of everyone. I know it's not a big deal, and it's not that I'm embarrassed about my body. I just like showering in private is all.

I've never been one of those girls who likes talking from stall to stall in the bathroom, either. When a group of girls go to a public restroom, conversation should cease once the stall doors close, in my opinion, and be resumed at the sinks or outside the restroom, once everyone's done peeing. But I know I'm in the minority on that.

Of course, my distaste for public showers means I'm now sitting in WooWoo waiting for my pizza and hoping that I don't stink so bad from cross-country that I'm ruining people's appetites.

"Hey, sorry I missed you at first in computer lab today," a male voice says from behind me. "I didn't realize you were in there or I'd have said hello earlier."

I look up in shock because I didn't hear Billy coming. He looks like he's about to start his shift. He walked in from the direction of the employee parking lot and he has his tie-dyed WooWoo apron looped over his arm and a backpack slung over his shoulder.

Plus, his glasses are on.

"Yeah, same here," I say. I smile, but mostly I'm hoping that he can't smell me. Maybe the pizza sauce odor hanging in the air will cover it. "I mean, I saw you, but I wasn't sure it was you at first. I didn't know you wore glasses. You don't wear them when you're here."

He drops his backpack onto the table and pulls out a hard-sided eyeglass case. "Can't. I'm leaning over the oven too much and they get steamed up." He takes off the glasses, puts them in the case, then says, "I mostly need them for reading, anyway. As long as I can tell a mushroom from a green pepper while I'm here, I'm good. So, um, you doing independent study fifth period?"

I nod. "History of the Middle East. You?"

"Advanced Physics."

Okay, I feel stupid.

"It's not as impressive as it sounds," he says, because my expression is clearly giving away my thoughts. "The beauty of independent study is that I can skip the painful stuff and do whatever's most interesting. It'd be worse if I actually had to take a class with a preset syllabus. I figure I'll get enough of that next year."

"You want to go to Colorado State, right?"

"Um, yeah." He pauses, then loops his backpack over his shoulder again. A very nice, broad shoulder—not that I'm really looking. "How'd you know?"

Because Rachel was listening to your behind-the-counter conversations, I'm tempted to say. But, instead, I shrug and tell him I think I heard him tell a coworker once when I was ordering pizza.

"Well, I'll find out soon enough. I'm pretty sure I'll get in." I get the feeling his grades are up there, and it's not like you need straight A's and a perfect SAT score to get into CSU, especially if you're a Colorado resident. He tells me he has an older sister who's a junior there, and since he goes up for the weekend every so often, he's really gotten to know the campus and has even made a few friends there.

"What about you?" he asks.

"I'm just a junior, so I've got a while to decide."

"Oh. I thought you were a senior, for some reason. You, um, you've been dating

77

Sean Norcross, right? I saw him here with you a couple of times over the summer. I haven't seen him in a while, though—it looks like you're mostly here with your friends. Is he in college now?"

He was paying attention to who I was here with?

"Nope, Sean's just a junior too." Billy clearly isn't too up on the social goings-on at school. I mean, it's a big school, so no one can know everyone, but Sean was pretty popular. Came with the football player–student council territory. "He moved to Connecticut."

"Oh. Sorry to hear that." I can tell from his face that he's not sure if he should say anything about being sorry we broke up. Maybe he doesn't know.

Or—I can't help but think for the sake of my own ego—maybe he's glad to hear Sean's gone, which means that I'm on the market. Not that I can picture Billy asking me out or anything.

And I *shouldn't*. Rachel technically scoped him out first.

"It's all right," I say. "People move, you know?"

The girl behind the counter waves at me to let me know my pizza's ready, so I stand up. "Guess I'll see you tomorrow?"

"Yeah, I gotta get behind the counter, anyway." He lowers his voice and adds, "She's probably dying to get out of here so she can go sit in her basement and smoke weed. I'm not going to hold her up."

I sneak a peek at the girl behind the counter, then look back at Billy. He's not exactly the type I figured could identify pot odor, but he's deadly serious. "I thought I smelled something when I was giving her my order."

"Wouldn't be surprised. She's new, but both times I've worked with her, I've smelled it. If she's not careful, she's going to get fired. Our boss doesn't stand for that kind of thing, especially if the customers can smell it on her. Five bucks says she's gone within a month."

I've seen the WooWoo owner. He's not the live-and-let-live type where pot's concerned, despite the fact that this place is very Boulder, what with all the tie-dye and the bright red tables inside and its location between a tattoo parlor and a Burton snowboard shop. If he even suspects that she's smoking pot in her off-hours, he'll can her. "I bet she doesn't make it a month. I bet she's gone by Saturday," I tell Billy.

He extends his hand and gives me a killer grin. "Five bucks?"

I shake on it, tell him I'll see him around, then go grab my pizza.

As I put the pie on the passenger seat of my Honda and pull out into traffic, it occurs to me that I've made new friends today for the first time in a long, long time. And better than with Eric, whom I've always kind of known, Billy's a male friend who's never been part of Sean's little circle. He runs with a whole different crowd, one I know nothing about, and who probably don't know all that much about me.

Even if he is Mr. Physics Geek, I think this is a Very Good Thing.

"Okay, give me the full report," Rachel says the second I pick up the telephone. "What classes is he taking? Is he just as hot out of the WooWoo uniform? And what's with him wearing glasses?"

"Hold on." I wave to Dad to let him know I'm taking the phone upstairs, and he shoos me out of the kitchen. Once I shut my bedroom door, I hook the phone so the receiver's balanced between my chin and ear and say, "Give me a second to concentrate. My legs are sore and I made the mistake of having three slices of pizza at dinner." I never eat three slices of WooWoo. The stuff is thick and supercheesy. It's like giving my stomach an engraved invitation to revolt when I shove that much grease in there.

"You had dinner at WooWoo?"

Whoops. Now she's really going to want details. "Nah, just picked it up for me and Dad. Probably shouldn't have. I'm trying not to have pizza more than once a week."

"Did you see him there?"

She sounds absolutely rabid. "Yeah, but only for a minute. The full report is that he needs glasses for reading and he takes 'em off at work because the pizza oven steams them up. He's also—hate to say it, Rachel—kind of a geek."

"No way."

"Oh, yeah. His independent study course? Take a wild guess."

She has no clue, so I tell her. I even describe the insanely detailed graphs and formulas he had written in his notebook, and the fact that when he's not in the standard-issue WooWoo white T-shirt, jeans, and tie-dyed apron, he's only a so-so dresser. Not a bad dresser at all, but not cutting edge like Rachel.

"Wow," she says, pausing to absorb it all. "No way could I ever go out with a guy who takes advanced physics of his own free will when he could do a zillion other things for independent study. One, how boring is that? And two, it means he's officially out of my league."

"Not out of your league," I assure her. "Just not your type, probably." And that's the honest truth. "Though you never know. Geek or not, he's pretty hot. And he's funny—I mean, look how he was when we talked at WooWoo and you asked about the name tag thing."

"True. But I'll continue to keep my eyes open, y'know?"

I know just whom she means. "So what

about the new guy who transferred in from Fort Collins?"

"Oh, now he very well might be in my league." I kick back against my pillows and grin as she describes how she managed to sit next to him at lunch today. I love just listening to her yak about this kind of thing. It makes me feel normal again. Like everything's going to be okay.

"Hey," she says on a long breath. "I just realized that I've been talking about guys—most of whom probably do not deserve the attention—for this entire phone call, and how rude that is, given what's been going on with you. I—"

"It's okay, Rachel." I keep my voice firm so she knows I really mean what I'm saying. "I think it's good for me. I like hearing this stuff. You'd tell me all this if Sean and I had never broken up, wouldn't you?"

"Yeah, but—"

"But nothin'. I don't want you treating me any different because of the whole Sean thing. That would make me feel worse. A lot worse. Got it?"

I can hear the smile in her voice. "Got it."

We chat for a little while longer—she tells me she's going to try to get a pass to computer lab so she can see Billy out of the WooWoo uniform and judge his geek factor for herself—then she finally admits that she's been procrastinating too long on getting her homework done and hangs up. For all her fashionista, guy-crazed tendencies, she's still careful about her grades. She just doesn't want anyone to know it. It's like it's her secret identity: Super Student.

I fold my legs under me, yoga-style, trying to get a good stretch in my quads. Maybe I need a secret identity too. Like Super Runner.

Amy will be thrilled if I become Super Runner. Well, after she tells me that she told me so. But it doesn't matter. I'll let her say it because I think this whole cross-country thing is going to work.

I mean, I'm still going to think about Sean. I'm still going to miss him—IMing him at all hours, sharing our little looks across history class. Sharing all my news and gossip with him. Listening to him describe how he took a blind hit at football practice or explain what really went on at a student council meeting.

And I'll definitely miss kissing him near the side door to the garage right before I go into my house at night, in the tiny space where I was certain Dad couldn't possibly see us. (I checked the vantage point from every window on that side of the house—I'm no dummy.)

But as much as I'll miss him, there was something about running today that made me feel like I don't *need* him.

Charlie Sheen would be proud.

Four

"Can anyone give me a summary of what Hrothgar says to Beowulf starting on this page? Or why it's so important to the story that it's come to be referred to as 'Hrothgar's Sermon'?" Mr. Whiddicomb is droning on, much like Hrothgar, about things that are apparent to anyone with half a brain.

Well, at least to anyone with half a brain who actually read all of *Beowulf*.

Why this epic poem dreck came to be considered such Great Literature that we've had to spend the first three weeks of school on it is beyond me. But my brain is still fumbling for something semi-intelligent to say, because with my luck this morning, he'll call on me. No matter how well I know the subject matter, I always sound like a dork when I actually get called on. Even though it's week three, I haven't said a word in this class yet, which means I'm due.

I hate, hate, hate having to talk in front of everyone.

When no one volunteers, he scans the room. His eyes land on me, but then he calls on Margot deVries, who, by sheer luck, is sitting on the opposite side of the room. And I know she'll run her mouth about characterization and the risks of *hubris* for as long as Mr. Whiddicomb will let her. She likes getting those participation points, even though she doesn't want to raise her hand and look too eager.

Since the coast is clear, I carefully unfold the piece of paper I printed out after checking my e-mail this morning and reread it.

I was feeling so good last night when I went to sleep—a combination of being totally high on running, now that I've officially made the team, and being totally wiped out from turning in a killer paper on the Five Pillars of Islam for independent study. (You want to know why it's so important to Muslims that they make a pilgrimage to Mecca? The reasons behind giving alms to the poor? Now I'm your girl.) And even though I managed to get sick to my stomach again during practice yesterday, I knocked fifteen seconds off my time. I woke up feeling excited about cross-country practice again today.

But the thing that really pushed me into a good mood? I figured out that I'm over Sean. Okay, not *over* over him. If he grabbed me right now and kissed me, the honest-with-myself part of me knows I'd kiss him back, just for the rush. But now that it's been nearly a month since his cut-and-run act, I've hit the point that thinking about him—or hearing from him—isn't going to make me as sick to my stomach as yesterday's cross-country run.

I know because I've been tested.

I glance over at Amy. She steals a look at Mr. Whiddicomb, then discreetly looks at the page I'm unfolding and raises an eyebrow. When Mr. Whiddicomb has his back turned, I stretch across the aisle to hand it to her. As her eyes skim the page, I mentally follow along with her, since I have every word memorized now. And I can tell that she's as stunned by what it says as I was when I first read it last night.

To: TnnsGrl@VVHSnet.edu
From: SeanNorx@freedommailct.com
Subject: Now that I'm in CT . . .

Hey, Chloe,
  Well, I know you'll probably hit the delete button without even reading this, but if you are reading it, please read to the end, okay?
  I just want to tell you that I'm sorry.
  I'm sorry I broke up with you at DIA. I'm sorry I did it the way I did it. I'm sorry that I gave a bunch of people my new e-mail addy but didn't give it to you. And I'm really sorry that I told a couple people about the breakup before you had a chance to. I assumed you would've told your friends, at least, but I still should have asked you first.
  And I'm sorry it's taken me so long to say I'm sorry. I just didn't know how.

Are you still reading?

Could you possibly forgive me?

Would it matter at all if I told you I still love you? That I still think you're scary beautiful, not to mention the best thing that ever happened to me?

Please write back.

Love,

—S

Amy looks over at me and mouths a creative variation on her favorite four-letter word.

I fake-whisper back, *I know!*

She flips over the paper and scrawls on it, then passes it back across the aisle.

This is unbelievable! I bet he wants to get back together because he realizes what a total ass he's been. I really do think he loves you. Are you going to forgive him? And can I say it again? UNBELIEVEABLE! P.S. Meant to tell you before class, but Rachel said she checked out WooWoo at the computer lab yesterday on a pass while you were in the library. She said he needs a day with some L.A. style expert I've never heard of for a clothing overhaul. Cracked me up! Think she'll try for Fort Collins guy now? Or get over her hang-ups and go for Billy anyway?

Mr. Whiddicomb picks that moment to start walking down my side of the room, waxing philosophical about Hrothgar, so I slide the e-mail under my notebook and try to look like I'm really involved in the story and everything he's saying. It's hard, though. None of this will be on a test—it's all just discussion to make sure we're covering the bases as we finish writing our papers on *Beowulf*, which we have to turn in on Monday.

Over the last couple years, I've figured out that if I focus my papers on the material I've actually paid attention to, ignore the rest, and make a convincing argument about why the part I'm discussing is important, I'll still get a pretty decent grade.

Another piece of paper comes flying across the aisle from Amy a few minutes later.

P.P.S. Sean really must be nervous about what you're going to say or he would have called, don't you think?

I glance over at her and shrug. I don't know what to think.

The instant the bell rings to end Torture 101 (a.k.a. honors English), Amy grabs me and scoots me into the hall ahead of everyone else so we have a few seconds of privacy. "Well?"

"Well what?"

She gives me the classic Amy Bellhorn eyeroll. "What are you going to do about the e-mail? Or did you already write back? Did you forgive him?"

"Connecticut's two hours ahead, so by the time I read it last night I'm sure he was asleep already."

I walk down the hall toward our lockers and try to play it casual, as if the e-mail from Sean isn't a big deal. I'm sure Amy knows better, though. I'm freaking out on the inside just as much as she is on the outside. "I figured since he won't check his e-mail until he knows I'm home from school, I'd be better off taking the day to decide what to say if I reply."

"If?!"

"Well, maybe I shouldn't, you know?"

Amy looks like she's going to elbow me

right into the wall. She takes a deep breath; then, in a voice she's clearly forcing to keep on the nice side, she says, "You went out with the guy for two and a half years, Chloe. He might've been a colossal jerk at the very end, but now he's apologizing for that. You can at least e-mail him back."

"I probably will." We turn the corner into junior hall, which is pretty crowded, so I lower my voice. "It's not a spite thing at all. It's that part of me thinks maybe I should leave well enough alone. If he does want to get back together—which I seriously doubt, or he would have just come out and said that in the e-mail—it's going to mean all kinds of emotional drama. And I don't want to deal with any more drama."

Or get my heart broken again. The hard truth is that, on the inside, I'm starting to realize that maybe Sean was right to break up with me. Not the way he did it, obviously, just the fact that he did it. In only three and a half weeks, I'm starting to feel like I haven't seen him in forever. What would it be like to wait two years for him, visiting on the occasional catch-as-catch-can holiday? Or for him to wait two years for me?

And that's *if* we end up going to the same college. We've always both assumed we'd be at the University of Colorado or at Colorado State (my preference, since that's where Dad went . . . Go, Rams!). But now that he's in Connecticut and won't have in-state tuition here anymore, why would he come back to the good ol' Centennial State? Just for me? How stupid a way to pick a school is that?

Maybe when he saw that MapQuest printout, he figured out something that I'm just now beginning to grasp—that as much as we really did love each other, it simply wasn't meant to be. At least not right now. Kind of like Rachel felt when she realized that WooWoo, while really a nice guy, probably has too many geek tendencies for her. I mean, she keeps checking him out, keeps making little noises about how cute he is, but I bet if she did a gut check, she'd realize it's not the right fit for her.

I can't explain this to Amy or to any of my other friends, though. They'll think

I'm being cold—that maybe I didn't really love Sean in the first place, which isn't the case at all.

I don't have to go to my locker, so I lean against the one next to Amy's. She lets out an attention-grabbing grumble as she turns the combination. "I don't get you, Chloe. I mean, yeah, no one wants to get her hopes up and then get crushed. But this is Sean. You guys had something special. You know he wouldn't have written that if he didn't want to get back together. You *know* it."

She stuffs a couple books in her backpack, shuts her locker door harder than necessary, then leans against it and stares at me. Her arms are crossed over her baby tee, making her biceps look bigger than normal, and her hair's in a braid straight down her back. It's her tough-girl, you'd-better-pay-attention-to-me pose. "Are you saying you absolutely, positively don't want to get back together, Chloe? Even after he said he still loves you? I think this is your only shot at it, so you shouldn't just blow it off."

"Sean wants to get back together?"

Kendra's voice comes from behind me. Great. "Did he call?"

"He e-mailed, but not necessarily to get back together," I say as I turn around. Rachel's with her too, so I hand them the piece of paper. "Here, read. But keep it quiet, okay? I don't want to be the focus of the rumor mill today. Sean's friends shouldn't hear about this unless Sean's the one to tell them, you know?" I don't want to be guilty of the same thing Sean did to me.

"Wow," Kendra says when she finishes reading. "He's practically begging! So what are you going to do?"

I give them the same spiel I gave Amy. Kendra nods and says, "Yeah, take your time and think. Do what's best for you."

But Rachel and Amy glance at each other, and I can tell instantly that Rachel agrees with Amy. She thinks I should give Sean a chance.

"I just need to let this gel in my brain," I say, taking the e-mail back from Kendra and slipping it into my backpack. "I'll probably reply when I get home from cross-country practice. There's a lot of time between now and then to figure out what I want to say."

The warning bell rings, so we start walking down the hall. Before Rachel ducks into her class, I ask her about Billy.

"I dunno," she says. "He's cute, but . . . well, we'll see." We make plans to meet at our usual table in the cafeteria for lunch, then Rachel adds, "And don't think talking about Billy's going to distract me from your Sean issues. Got it?"

"Gotcha."

As Amy and Kendra speed up to get to their next class—a couple doors past where I need to go—and they start whispering back and forth, I get the feeling that the rumor mill's going to start spinning whether I want it to or not.

"You look wiped," Billy says as we settle down in front of our computers during fifth period. After the first few days of sitting across the computer lab from each other, I moved over to an empty seat next to his, under the row of windows.

It felt stupid—after we chatted that afternoon in WooWoo following my first cross-country practice—for me to sit by myself and leave him sitting by himself in independent study. So after a couple days of feeling awkward, smiling at each other but not sitting together, I just decided to pick up my stuff and move. And it hasn't felt awkward since.

"It's been a long day," I tell him as I yank out the folder full of notes I used to write my paper on the Five Pillars. My goal for today is to get all the random notes organized and put away, and then to write up a bibliography of the reading I need to do for my next paper. All the little "see how productive I'm being?" things that keep Mrs. Berkowski happy she sponsored me for this class.

Of course, my other goal for the hour is to shut out Rachel's and Amy's voices in my head, telling me for the entire freaking lunch hour that it can't hurt to give Sean a second chance. I finally blew up and told Rachel that if she's so hot for Sean, she should e-mail him and ask him out.

I've never seen Rachel so shocked. Her face—always pale—went totally white when I said it.

Of course I immediately apologized. And I mean a big-time apology. She was understanding and told me it was just stress, no biggie, and Kendra told Rachel it was no wonder I popped off, what with all the pressure she and Amy were putting on me about Sean. Even though we left on a note of happy-happy-joy-joy, all I could think was that in the future maybe I should keep my e-mails from Sean to myself.

Billy smiles and slides a pack of cinnamon gum toward me. I grab a piece and push it back. It's become our little ritual, since fifth period's right after lunch and we both need to conquer cafeteria breath. The whole share-a-pack thing somehow makes me feel better.

"How'd your test go?" Even though I designed my independent study to be mostly papers, he doesn't get off so easy, taking advanced physics. Every few weeks he has to go pick up an exam from the teacher who helped him design his class.

"Not so bad." He aims, then shoots his foil gum wrapper into the trash can at the end of the row. "He didn't have it graded when I stopped by at lunch, so I'll find out for sure tomorrow. I'm just glad it's over. I can take it easy for a few weeks."

"I hear you there." I'm off the hook too, now that I turned in my first paper.

It's peaceful in here, with the sun coming in through the windows and the constant tapping of fingers on keyboards behind us. No worries about being called on or being hit with a pop quiz. Billy and I are the only people doing independent study this period, so we're the only two people who are in here for fifth period every day. The rest are just floaters, people with the random pass to the computer lab. Since the monitor is used to us by now and she's figured out that we actually do get work done, she doesn't say anything if Billy and I talk quietly while we're here. Lately she's been skipping our row when she does her walk-through Internet porn checks.

Today, even though it's nice in here, we both decide that we'd be more productive in the library, since neither one of us needs to do much computer work. We grab passes and on the way out we start talking about the latest from last night's television shows. We're both totally into this new show called *Southie*, about a group of teenagers who live in Boston.

"I missed the first ten minutes," he says. "I got hung up at WooWoo. Oh, and you owe me five bucks. Told you Colleen and Kyle wouldn't get together this week."

I fish a fiver out of my pocket—I had it ready 'cause I knew he'd ask—and grumble about how shows draw out these relationships way longer than they should, just to get ratings. It's wrong how the previews are such a tease.

He stuffs the five in his wallet. "Consider it payback for when you won the bet about Pothead Girl."

"I knew she'd get fired fast." I can't help but remind him about it every so often. It felt good to win that bet. Not because of the money—just because it's fun to laugh and joke around with a normal guy. One who isn't Sean—or, like Eric Biedermeyer, a friend of Sean's.

One who's *my* friend. And who I know won't nag me about Sean in any way, shape, or form. Or worse, e-mail Sean and tell him what I've been up to.

"So, you have plans this weekend?"

"Not really," I say. "I mean, it's pretty early to know what's going on. My dad said something about trying to get Nuggets tickets for Friday night, but that was a couple weeks ago, so I'm not sure he's serious about it. And our first cross-country meet's on Saturday morning."

"You ready?"

"Think so," I lie. Envisioning it puts my gut in a knot. I'm used to competition from tennis, but for some reason, this feels different. I've been playing tennis all my life, so I guess it's 'cause I can show up for a match, play on autopilot, and still do pretty well. I'm not at that point with cross-country.

We get to the library, show our passes, then find a quiet table near the back. After I locate the books I need and return to my seat, Billy whispers, "About cross-country? I think it's really great that you went out. I mean, as a junior. That took guts."

"No, it took Amy harassing me." I know I sound sarcastic, so I shoot him a smile to let him know it's cool. Secretly, I'm thrilled that he thinks I have guts. "But you know what I think is cool? The fact that you're doing all that"—I point toward his notebook, which has even more scribbles and formulas in it than usual—"and that you like it. Even if you play it off sometimes. What is it you're doing there, anyway?"

"Promise not to laugh?"

"Of course."

"You know how the speed of light is a constant?"

I nod, 'cause I s'pose that's true, though I haven't really thought about it.

"Well, someday I want to prove that it's not. A constant, that is."

I blink. "So all of this stuff you're working on . . . it's not for class?"

"Some of it is. But the speed of light stuff, no. I just know my sponsor would laugh at me."

Okay, Billy is freaking brilliant. "Well, then your sponsor's the dumb one. I think it's really cool you want to do that. I mean, you could win a Nobel prize or something for that, right?"

One side of his mouth hooks up into a completely sexy geek grin. "You'd think. But I want to do it just to do it, you know?"

A group of juniors come in and grab a table that's two over from ours, including a couple of the nicer cheerleaders and a girl who was on student council with Sean last year, so I give them a wave and a "Hey."

They all smile back, but there's something uncomfortable in the way they're looking at me. Or, more precisely, the way they're looking at me and Billy. Like they think it's bizarre that we're sitting together.

I ignore them and go back to talking with Billy about the speed of light. I don't get a thing he's saying, but I'm entertained by the fact that he gets it. It's all very *Star Trek* of him, but in a good way.

We finally get to work, but pretty soon, Billy whispers so only I can hear, "You can go sit with them if you want."

"I'm fine." I go back to my Five Pillars notes for a sec, but then find myself glancing up at him because I can't get his comment out of my head. "Wait. Why would you say that?"

Deadpan, he says, "'Cause you're pretty."

I straighten up in my chair, then lean across the table and whisper. "I'm not sure if you just complimented me or if I'm supposed to take offense."

This elicits a grin. "No offense. It's just that . . . well, girls like you usually hang out with girls like them. The Beautiful People. And they were looking at you in a way that said, *Move your butt over here and stop talking about science,* you know?"

I'm not quite sure how to take what he's saying, but I can tell he's not trying to piss me off.

"Look, can I tell you something, Chloe?"

I shrug. "Go right ahead."

"I don't know if you realize it, but you're different from them. I mean that in a good way. I like Rachel and Kendra and Amy. They're always nice to me at the pizza place, even if they seem to forget who I am when we're in school—"

"That's not fair." In Rachel's case, for sure. "We didn't even know you went to our school until a few weeks ago. Most people who hang at WooWoo live in Boulder. Plus, you're a senior. You're not exactly in class with us."

Even though I'm feeling defensive, I give him what I'm hoping is a devious-looking grin. "And you have that whole Clark Kent thing going with the glasses."

"And the advanced physics. And the fact I go my own way." He smiles so only one side of his mouth goes up. "And that's kind of my point. I'm in one social class, and the girls at the table over there are in another. Your friends are far nicer to me than that crowd ever would be, but you and your friends still worry about their opinions." He tips his head subtly in the direction of the juniors. "Not that—"

I raise an eyebrow. "Are you about to say, 'Not that there's anything wrong with that'?"

"Very funny." He leans forward, and for a split second, I realize that I'm attracted to him. Like, *really* attracted to him. There's that feeling of being unable to breathe all the way down into my lungs when his blue eyes lock with mine.

How did that happen?

How did this go from a he's-a-cool-guy to an omigod-I-want-him-now thing? Because at this moment, I do, even though I'm pretty sure I should be offended by what he's saying.

Okay, this is *not* happening. I've gotta get over it.

He whispers, "All I'm saying is that we're different in a lot of ways. I have nerd tendencies. I know that. And even though you're much nerdier on the inside than you let on to the world and you're comfortable hanging out on your own—or just with me—because of the fact you're smokin' hot and your friends aren't too shabby either, the four of you tend to run with the Beautiful People. You, Amy, Kendra, and Rachel, I mean. You usually sit near all the 'in' people at basketball games and in the cafeteria. You sometimes act like you don't care about your grades any more than it takes to get into wherever it is you want to go to college because that's the cool thing to do when you're around that crowd. You and your friends care about what the popular crowd thinks of you, even if you don't really want to hang with them . . . probably because they do treat people like me as if we're invisible."

I'm about to interrupt, but he continues, "Anyway—my long-winded point is that I was offering you the chance to sit with the cool people instead of with Geek Boy, because I thought it was the polite move."

"That's a huge bunch of assumptions you're making," I tell him. "Huge."

Okay, so I do care about what the cheerleader–student council–popular types think. Even, and maybe especially, Margot deVries. Doesn't everyone? I don't want to piss them off because I don't want to be on the bad end of gossip and be the center of attention, like after the "you could model" incident. With Rachel, it's probably because she wants them to respect her and the fact that she's completely up on the latest styles and trends, even if she doesn't want to be their best bud or anything. Ditto with Amy and her athletic ability, and Kendra with her Zen-like wisdom. We all just want to be valued for who we are. But I would never ditch him to go sit with them.

He jams his hands into his wavy, sun-bleached hair. His voice is still low, so the girls at the other table can't hear as he says, "I can tell you're taking what I'm saying all wrong. I *like* your friends. I do. And I'm not saying one crowd is better than another. It just is what it is."

He glances at the ceiling for a second, then looks back at me. "You're smart and you're curious, or you wouldn't be doing history of the Middle East and really enjoying it. You're witty and you're kind to everyone you meet, no matter who they are. I should have known better than to assume you'd want to switch seats. If you really wanted to be one of them, you could be. Anytime."

I can't help but smile. I try to hide it by looking down, but I can't.

He smiles back—a smile that reaches all the way to his eyes, making them crinkle at the corners—and says, "I guess the better I get to know you, the more I'm finding that any assumptions I'd make about you based on looks alone are all wrong. And I'm sorry."

"Just like assumptions you think people make about you being a geek are all wrong." I take a deep breath. I know I could probably get really torqued if I picked apart his words and analyzed them, but I can tell from the intensity of his look that what he's really trying to tell me is that he likes me for me and that he realizes I'm not as shallow as we both perceive the popular crowd to be. And that there's a vibe between us that we both know is out of the ordinary.

I just wish I knew whether he thinks it's a we-could-be-more-than-friends vibe.

Man, what is *with* me?!

"Anyway, I know what you're really trying to say," I finish. "And it's sweet."

Because the thing is, even though I don't really like what he assumes about me making nice-nice with the Beautiful People, it's true of the world at large. Pretty girls tend to hang out with other pretty girls. The goths hang out with other goths, the geeks with geeks, the religious kids with other religious kids, and so on. It just is what it is.

But I've always struggled to prove to everyone that I'm more than my looks, which Mr. Science Geek has to know are simply the result of a lucky draw from the gene pool. And other than Sean and my small group of supertight girlfriends, he's the first person to figure out I'm not stupid or lacking personality simply because I'm pretty. That I care about things like the history of the Middle East.

"But from now on," I tell him, "if I'm sitting with you, it's because I want to sit with you. And I'm going to assume that if you're sitting with me, it's because you want to sit with me. Got it?"

"Got it. And I hereby promise not to ditch you for the pocket protector or Dungeons & Dragons crowds as long as you don't ditch me for the prom king. Oh, and as long as you never, ever again call me 'sweet.' I'm not sweet, believe me."

"Deal. But . . . um, does anyone really play Dungeons & Dragons anymore?"

"I have no clue. And I don't know anyone who actually owns a pocket protector either."

I give him a look I know is flirty, even though I really shouldn't. And even though I know I suck at flirting and probably would die of embarrassment if I could see myself in a mirror. "That's a relief."

On that, we get to work, since both of us actually do have to show that we've accomplished something every day. A few minutes before the bell's due to ring, he looks up at me and says, "I think, even though you'd probably never admit it, that you like to do your own thing more than your friends do. Maybe it's that you're an only child, or that your dad pretty much treats you like an adult. But whatever it is, I think it's really cool."

"Thanks, that's—"

"Don't call me sweet."

"I'm not!" I say, trying not to laugh since the library monitor would be over in a heartbeat.

I put the books I used back on their shelves, one by one, cradling the armload so I don't drop them. But when I move from row to row in the stacks, it's like I can feel the girls at the other table watching me. I'm not sure if it's my imagination, though. When I turn around to go back to my table, they're all talking quietly and loading up their backpacks.

I'm freaking myself out here.

"I forgot," Billy says when I get back to the table and start arranging my books in my backpack. "I asked you on the way down here what you were doing this weekend. Well, I had a reason. I know it's early to plan, but I was hoping you could come over Saturday night. My sister's coming home from college for the weekend and we thought it'd be fun to have a couple people over to play poker. Just a casual kind of thing—no heavy stakes. What do you think?"

What do I think?!

"Let me check with my dad and I'll get back to you tomorrow." But even as I say it, I know I want to go. It might be casual to Billy, but it feels like an adventure to me. A chance to prove something to myself.

When the bell rings, I toss my backpack over my shoulder and say, "You can plan on me being there. I'm sure it won't be a problem."

Composing one lousy e-mail has taken me nearly an hour. It's the best I can do, but now I'm staring at it and wondering whether I have the guts to click on the send button.

To: SeanNorx@freedommailct.com
From: TnnsGrl@VVHSnet.edu
Subject: RE: Now that I'm in CT . . .

Hi Sean,

1) Of course I didn't delete your
e-mail. I read it all.

2) You're forgiven. On all counts. I was
pretty angry, I'll admit. But I'm over it
now.

3) I know what you did at DIA wasn't
easy. Neither was apologizing for it. But in
the long run, I realize that you were right.
I don't know how anyone—even
people as into each other as we've been the
past couple years—who can sustain a relationship from all the way across the country. At least not without owning
private jets or something.

4) What's important is that we'll always
respect each other and have a special
place in each other's hearts.
Always,
Chloe

I just can't hit send. I wonder if I'm being
lame, saying all that stuff about sustaining a

relationship. It feels very Teen Angst Movie of the Week. Even though I've rewritten item number four a zillion times, I can't think of a better way to say it. I can't bring myself to say that I love him back. Maybe I do, but it's changed. I don't want to lead him on if Rachel and Amy are right (which I admit, they probably are) and he wants to get back together.

I mean, if I really loved him, would I be feeling at all attracted to Billy? Or scoping out other guys as I walk through the halls? Not that I'm *scoping* scoping—like Rachel does when she goes to the mall or anything— but when I've talked to guys the last couple weeks, even if it's just to ask what page we're on in class or to work on an experiment in chemistry lab, there's a different feel to it than before.

Like I have possibilities I was too blind or too content to see.

I never used to get that feeling—that feeling that talking to a guy, any guy, is different from talking to the girls—at least not while I was with Sean. But I do now, and I figure it's best if I'm just honest with myself about it.

I mouse over the send button, reread the

whole thing, then decide not to click. Instead, I cut and paste the message into a separate document and save it, then delete the actual e-mail, just to be certain I don't fire it off accidentally. Maybe I'll send it tomorrow.

Maybe not.

At two in the morning, I tiptoe over to the computer and open the document. Without reading it again (because, really, I don't have to), I copy it, paste it back into an e-mail, then send it as is. Done. *Finito.* Let the chips fall where they may.

Five minutes later, just as I'm drifting off to sleep, I mentally kick myself. As soon as he opens it, Sean's going to see from the time stamp that I sent my reply at two a.m.

He's going to think I've been staying awake stressing about him and overanalyzing every word of what I wrote.

He'll be right, but still . . .

To: SeanNorx@freedommailct.com

From: TnnsGrl@VVHSnet.edu

Subject: Fwd: RE: Now that I'm in CT . . .

Hi Sean,

I tried to reply to your e-mail last night before I went to bed, but I think my server was acting up. I'm not sure if it ever delivered the reply. I'm forwarding it at the end of this
message. If you end up getting this twice, sorry. Computer burps and all.

Always,

Chloe

Five

"It's more blunt than I thought you'd be," Kendra says between bites of pizza, now that I've been badgered into telling everyone word-for-word (twice) what I wrote back to Sean. "But I think you did the right thing. It sounds like you wrote it in a way that isn't rude or embarrassing but that clearly lets him know you're not interested in getting back together."

I thank her for being so supportive, then look across the table toward Amy and Rachel. Their looks aren't so supportive. In fact, they're glaring at me. Especially Rachel. "I just don't get it," she says.

Amy lets out a snarky, annoyed grunt.

Although she's theoretically my best friend and should be the one person at the table who's in my corner, she's not at all. "You honestly want to be broken up with Sean now? After being so depressed right after the whole scene at DIA?"

I lift one shoulder, then let it drop. I explained myself yesterday when I got Sean's e-mail.

Frankly, I think that given their reaction (well, at least Amy's and Rachel's), it was really nice of me to ask them to meet me for dinner after cross-country so I could tell them how I handled it. I mean, I hate when everyone analyzes me and my personal life. When I was with Sean, it was just a given that everything was good in my world. I was able to laugh and joke around without having every single action I made picked apart. Now, not so much.

"Whoa." Rachel's eyes get really big. "Are you all hot for someone else?"

"No, not really," I answer automatically, but I'm thinking about Billy even as the denial leaves my mouth, which I know is insane. It's probably just 'cause I'm sitting in a booth at WooWoo and I haven't been here with the girls in a couple weeks. And I wouldn't have come here today—not since I knew we'd be talking about my personal life—if I hadn't known for sure that he didn't have to work tonight.

"'Not really'?" Amy asks.

They're all staring at me, so I feel compelled to explain. "Being single again has opened my eyes. Maybe there's someone else out there for me. Someone better than Sean. But since I've been living in Sean World for the last couple of years, how would I know?"

Amy addresses the whole table as if I'd never spoken. "I think 'not really' means there *is* someone Chloe's been lusting after. Or a couple someones."

I set my Diet Pepsi on my napkin so it doesn't make a ring. "Geez, even if I am looking at other guys—and I'm not saying that I am—is that illegal?"

The minute the remark leaves my mouth, I get the impression that, in their minds, it kinda is.

"Look," I say carefully. "All I'm saying is that maybe I need some time not being Sean's girlfriend. I was totally honest in my e-mail to him. I don't think we could have made the long-distance thing work. Not for very long. So why beat my head against the wall over it?"

Kendra, smarty person that she is, manages to say something totally noncommittal, then change the subject by asking Rachel about Fort Collins Guy—whose real name is Pete. "Tell them what you told me," Kendra adds.

"Well, you guys know he's in my chemistry class, right?"

We nod, because of course we've heard it a zillion times since school started.

"Well, we had a lab today, and he was at the lab table behind me, so we talked some." Rachel's mouth twists into a catlike smile, and she wraps a blond curl around one finger. "He asked if I wanted to catch a movie on Saturday. It's with a group of people, but I still think that's a good sign. He obviously wants me to hang out with him and his friends, which means he must want to get to know me better. Oh, and you guys know that astonishingly gorgeous senior named Jake? He's on the basketball team. I think his last name starts with a *D*?"

"Driscoll," we all say at once. Even though it's a big school, you get to know the names of the really hot guys pretty fast, because everyone talks about them.

"Well, Fort Collins Guy is apparently pretty tight with Gorgeous Jake, so Jake's coming along too."

"Total score for you!" Kendra says.

"No kidding," Amy says through a bite of pizza.

Rachel suddenly sits up straight. I follow her gaze and see that Billy's heading our way. He's in his tie-dye, stopping at nearby tables offering to refill drinks. We're clearly in his path. I take a deep breath, trying not to show how shocked I am. He told me in class today that he was finally getting a day off.

"And there's always WooWoo. Even if he's a little geekier than I thought, he's still a hottie." Rachel's voice turns silky as she looks in Billy's direction. "So you know, lots of possibilities. I think I'm going to have a very good junior year."

Alarms are ringing in my head. Is Rachel really serious about being interested in Billy? I thought she'd decided to scratch him off her list after she checked him out in his natural habitat at the computer lab.

Rachel grins at Amy, and Amy bites her lip. Then Kendra smiles at both of them and I wonder what big secret I'm missing. Amy grabs a napkin from the dispenser and says, "I'm not telling you, Rachel, so lay off."

"No way."

I want to ask Rachel if Billy's really her type, but Amy looks like she just swallowed a cockroach with her slice, so I frown at her. "Um, what's going on?"

"Amy has a crush on someone," Rachel singsongs.

"So, this afternoon at softball, I hit one over the left field fence," Amy says in an attempt to change the topic. She even turns in the booth so her back is to Rachel, who's sitting next to her. "You know how I never pull left, always to center or right? So the coach is having me change my whole stance. See if I can take advantage of that short left field fence."

I love this move, because it's just so Amy. And also because I know she'll tell me later, when it's just the two of us, if she really does have it bad for someone new. She flirts with a lot of guys, but when she's really interested in someone, she gets very private about it. And usually the one guy she likes is the one she absolutely can't flirt with. She gets too nervous to function.

Thank goodness Kendra and Rachel have never noticed that little factoid or they'd be able to figure out who she's crushing on pretty fast.

To help her out, I say, "Really? Can you change where you're hitting the ball that much just by changing your stance?"

"Sure." Amy's smile is so perky it's all I can do not to fall apart laughing. "No different from tennis."

"Wow, like, that's amaaa-zing!"

Since we're being completely fake, Rachel's rolling her eyes, but Kendra looks up just as Billy gets to our table.

"Hey guys, how's it going? Please don't tell me you need drink refills, all right?"

"You're safe with us," Amy assures him. Billy's hit all the other tables and doesn't have to go anywhere right away, so we all start gossiping about the PE teacher, since the word around school is that she's pregnant (a juicy bit of info if true, since she's recently divorced).

Eventually, I say to Billy, "What are you doing here, anyway? I thought you weren't working today."

"Someone called in sick." He shrugs, adding, "I wasn't planning on doing anything other than vegging out in front of the TV, so I figured I should come in and make a few extra bucks."

Rachel changes the subject and asks him questions about how he did in chemistry and how tough the grading is on the labs, since Billy (certified brain) took it as a sophomore two years ago. I follow along at first, but after a few minutes, I'm only half listening. Then Rachel leans closer to him, touching his shirt sleeve. At that moment, it suddenly hits me that I don't want Rachel to flirt with him.

I like Billy.

Well, not in a head-over-heels, rabid crush, I-can't-control-myself-around-him obsessive kind of way. But there's definitely an attraction that's stronger than the quickie rush I felt in the library. The one I thought maybe I imagined.

Now I know I didn't.

Also, as Billy laughs at something Rachel says, it occurs to me that—aside from any possible feelings I might have for Billy—they'd get along fine if they went out, but it wouldn't last. They're just too different. Rachel would always be looking for the Next Perfect Guy, while Billy strikes me as the more serious, long-term type. I would hate to see either of them hurt. If they got together, it'd definitely screw up one of them, if not both.

I shove the thought out of my head and jump back into the conversation for a while—not that I can really jump in. Rachel's yakking like mad to Billy, as if the rest of us aren't even here. Pretty soon, Amy starts cleaning up the crumbs from the table and making a show of putting her napkin on her paper plate.

After another couple minutes of chemistry talk, Amy interrupts to say she has to head home so she can get started on this big assignment she has for French. Finally, Rachel takes the hint and stands up, since Amy's her ride. And—if I had to bet—because she ran out of chemistry-related questions for Billy that don't make her motives look totally obvious.

"I'm still eating, but you two go ahead," Kendra says. I figure I should stay a few minutes so Kendra won't be sitting here by herself, but I really want to get home so I can call Amy and see what the deal is with her theoretical crush. I'm just about to stand up, when Kendra elbows me. Hard.

I glance at her, then say, "I'll stay for a little while too. Keep Kendra company." I turn and give Amy a look that lets her know I'll call her, and she nods back before saying good-bye.

In the shuffle of backpacks, Billy grabs their empty plates, tells us he'll swing by our table again if he gets the chance, then heads up to the counter.

Once we're alone, Kendra slides her plate to the other side of the booth so we can spread out. As soon as she's seated again, she says, "So who is it?"

"Who's what?"

"When you said 'not really' about having it bad for someone. Who is it?"

I close my eyes for a second. She bruised my ribs with her pointy elbow for this?

Amy I'd expect to batter me, not Kendra. Not unless she thought it was important.

"It's no one," I tell her, completely straight-faced. "Seriously. I just know that as much as I loved Sean, there's no way we can stay together for two years while he's in Connecticut, meeting new people and getting hit on by who-knows-how-many girls while I'm here in Colorado, living the same-old, same-old life."

She drops her napkin over the uneaten pizza slice she took when Amy and Rachel were leaving. "Chloe, I really meant it when I said I thought you did the right thing with Sean. It's just . . ." She pauses, glances toward the counter, then leans in. "I'm asking because your life isn't the same-old, same-old. You're doing new things. Hanging out with us more. And I think you're meeting new people, too. Like Billy."

"I met Billy before Sean left—"

"Sort of. You know him a lot better now."

There's a mushroom sitting all by its lonesome at the edge of the pizza pan, so I snag it with my index finger and thumb and pop it in my mouth, vaguely wondering if it counts toward my government-recommended five fruits and veggies a day. "Well, of course. We have independent study together."

"I think it's more than that. When you said that to him, about being surprised he was working today . . . I don't know. I think there's something about the way you two look at each other and talk. You're very comfortable together. And when he said he'd try to get back to our table again, he looked straight at you."

I forage for more mushrooms, even though I'm stuffed, just to buy myself a minute to think.

Kendra's voice is soft. "You like him, don't you, Chloe?"

As soon as my mouth's empty, I say, "Billy and I are friends. That's it. There is absolutely nothing going on with us."

She just keeps looking at me, so I say, "Look, can you keep this to yourself?"

"Depends on what 'this' is."

"Oh, that's reassuring."

She steals a look out the window, where Amy's car is now pulling into traffic, then focuses on me again. "Fine, fine. I'll keep my mouth shut."

Still not very reassuring, but Kendra's usually pretty good at not spilling secrets. Choosing my words carefully, I tell her, "Billy's really cool, so I think I *could* like him. We have a great time in Independent Study, just hanging out and talking about everything. But I don't want to step on Rachel's turf if she's really interested. So I'm not going to do anything about it. Besides, even if there wasn't a Rachel issue, I don't know if I'm ready to get serious about anyone right now."

"But?" She glances toward the pizza counter, where Billy's busy taking down a huge order for a group of CU guys in fraternity sweatshirts.

I must look nervous as hell, because she clearly knows there's more going on than I'm saying. "But . . . he asked me if I wanted to come over to his house this Saturday. *Not* as a date—totally not—just to play poker with him and his sister and some of his sister's friends. I guess she's coming home from CSU this weekend."

"Well, if there's nothing going on, how come you didn't say anything?"

The accusation in her voice pisses me

off, but I try to keep my cool. "It's not that it's any big secret. Really."

"So?"

"So Rachel and Amy will read all sorts of things into it because of the Sean e-mail. They'll think I'm saying no to Sean because of Billy—and I'm not. I'm saying no to Sean because I know it's over between us."

In my gut, I know I've kept quiet because I don't want to piss off Rachel. But now that the Sean-versus-Billy explanation comes out of my mouth, I realize it's the truth. I don't want Sean anymore. Billy or no Billy.

Kendra leans back in the booth and sits sideways, leaning against the window and putting her feet up on the bench. "You're probably right," she admits. "For whatever reason, they really want you to stay with Sean. Rachel especially."

"Gee, you think so?" I say, laughing this time.

She makes a face and tells me she doesn't get their fixation with me and Sean, then reaches under her napkin to pick at her pizza. After a couple bites, she says, "I still think you need to tell Rachel about going over to Billy's. Make it completely clear that it's a friend thing, and that Billy's sister will be there with a bunch of her friends. Otherwise, when Rachel hears about it, she's going to think you're keeping it a secret for some reason. And you know she will, at some point."

I know why Kendra's saying this, but part of me worries that Rachel still won't understand. Normally she would—she's the type who really likes informal, just-friends get-togethers like Billy's sister is having, for one, so she'd get that it's not a date thing. And for two, even if I told her that I was totally crushing on Billy, Rachel still wouldn't hold it against me unless there was actually something official going on between the two of them and she thought I was out-and-out trying to steal him or something. She and Kendra both liked the same guy for a while freshman year, and when he ended up asking out Kendra, Rachel just shrugged and started scoping out her next victim. She's very Charlie Sheen-esque that way.

But the timing of the Sean e-mail will throw everything I might say about Billy just being a friend into doubt, and then she just might think I'm lying about the whole thing, that it's not just a simple poker night.

I explain all this to Kendra, and she agrees that it's a risk. "But I still think you should say something. She'll be out with Fort Collins Pete and that Gorgeous Jake guy and all their friends on Saturday night, anyway. So you can always say you'd have thought about asking her along, but—"

"No, I'm not going to lie about it. Besides, Billy asked me before I knew about Pete and Jake." I exhale and push away the pizza. I'm burning off a lot of calories at cross-country, but no one burns off this many in a day.

"Then tell her exactly what you told me."

I nod. "Yeah, that's probably the best thing to do."

I'm going to have to. I just wish I could keep it to myself a while longer. I have no idea where this is going with Billy—*if* this is even a thing, since the vibe I'm feeling may be my own wishful thinking—but I kind of liked having it to myself.

"You're way too perceptive, you know," I tell Kendra. "You're killing me."

She laughs aloud. "Not that perceptive. I have no idea who Amy's interested in. Do you?"

This time, I tell her that I honestly don't, then add, "I just hope it's not Billy."

"So spill," I say to Amy a couple hours later. I watched TV with Dad, then managed to get halfway through a nasty trig assignment before calling Amy to work through one of the harder problems. Of course, the second she helped me figure it out, I told her I needed the answer to the real question—who it is she's interested in.

"Why does everyone think I'm after someone in particular?" she whines.

"Everyone doesn't. Just Rachel. And since you didn't deny it, now Kendra and I are wondering. But believe me, you're safe from the mass 'everyone' for now."

"Everyone except the ones who really matter," she retorts.

"Look, if you don't want to tell me, that's cool." More than ever, I understand the need for privacy in this area.

"It's not that I don't want to tell you."

"So there is somebody?"

"Yeah." She doesn't sound too happy about it, though. "I'd kind of been thinking about him all summer, but ever since school started, it's like he's taking over my brain. Isn't that crazy? You know I'm usually able to distract myself from guy issues, pulling that whole Charlie Sheen routine you keep talking about, but this time—"

"*Who*, Amy? If we talk it over, maybe we can figure out a way to get him interested back." Geez, but she's full of drama tonight. "You know you can always tell me this stuff and I'll keep it in the confidential file."

There's a pause, then she says, "It's just . . . well, things feel different now. I always knew I was safe coming to you with this kind of thing because you were with Sean, so there was never this sense, like I've always had with Rachel and Kendra, of . . . oh, I dunno." A rush of breath comes over the phone line. "I'm just being silly, I guess. I'm not good at this girly stuff."

"No, it's okay. I understand. I'm learning that I'm not very good at it either."

Because I was the one in a rock-solid relationship, all three of my friends have looked to me for impartial advice at one time or another. Probably because they thought I had some secret to landing a boyfriend. Or else they knew I had no interest in whomever it was they liked. While the no-interest part was true, I certainly never had any great insight into how to land the right guy. In my case, it just kind of happened.

Of course, now I'm also wondering if her hesitation is because she thinks her mystery crush is someone I might be interested in.

"You'd understand? Really?" Amy sounds skeptical.

"Yeah, really. But if you decide to tell me, you know I'll keep it to myself. Same as always."

"I know you will. Oh, and thanks for covering my tail at WooWoo today with the where-to-hit-the-ball discussion. You know that was just a monster load of purple pig—"

"I figured," I say, cutting off her favorite obscenity midway.

She gets quiet for a second, and I can tell she's trying to work out how she wants to tell me whatever-it-is, so I just wait.

"Here's the thing," she finally says. "I think he likes someone else. So before I say anything—to anyone—I just want to wait and see if he's really interested in the person I think he's interested in. If not, then I'll do something about it."

Oooo-kay. Exactly what I'd hoped not to hear. "And you think you'll know this soon?"

"Yeah. It's someone I see a lot—both the guy and the person I think he's interested in—and the two of them see more of each other than they used to, just 'cause of how school stuff panned out this year, so . . . well, I'll probably know soon. I just don't want to say anything, in case they do get together."

I get a sinking feeling in my stomach as she's talking, and I can't help but ask, "Um, Amy? Is it Billy?"

"No way. No! I mean, he's cool, but he doesn't do a thing for me." She lets loose a total belly laugh. "Could you imagine? I'd break that boy."

She's probably right about that. "Well,

I know you generally go for the independent types or the superjocks, but I still thought I'd ask."

"Ohhhhh, because of Rachel! I get it." She utters an interesting variation of her fave swear word, and I tease her for being my foulmouthed friend. I'm also extremely relieved because I can tell she means it about not liking Billy. But then she adds, "You know I'd never scam a guy Rachel's had her eye on, even if I did like him. Which I don't."

"Well, how serious is Rachel about Billy, do you think?" I'm proud of myself for asking this in a way that doesn't make it sound the least bit like I'm interested in him, even though guilt is starting to eat at me.

"Who knows? Probably not very. You know Rachel. But it's the principle of the thing."

"Yeah, guess that's true." I am in so much trouble.

I have got, *got* to get out of going to Billy's Saturday. Somehow. Though even as I think it, another part of me thinks no, I *should* go. He invited me, I said yes. It'd be rude to back out now, especially when I really don't have a valid excuse like having a root canal or something like that. Plus, it's just a friendly thing, even if I am attracted to him.

Then Dad starts yelling from downstairs, "Hey, Chloe, off the phone!"

"Was that your dad?" Amy asks.

"Who else? Probably needs to make a call for work."

"You wanna call me back on your cell?"

I glance at the clock. It's nearly nine, which is more likely the reason Dad's yelling. "I'm only halfway through the trig homework."

"Ouch."

"Plus I should look at chemistry. Mr. Schneider keeps dropping hints about a pop quiz, and I have a nasty feeling it'll be tomorrow. Fridays seem to be the day."

"You're probably right. Hope Ms. Cooper doesn't have one too. Yuck."

We say our good-byes, and then I yell to Dad that I'm off the phone. I start to study the formula for molar volume so I don't bomb a potential pop quiz (who decided a "mole" should be a unit of measurement? I must ask), but I keep replaying Kendra's and Amy's words in my head.

Kendra clearly thinks I should tell Rachel.

On the other hand, Amy would probably tell me to keep quiet and not do anything, like she's doing with whoever it is she has a crush on.

When I do a nonemotional, totally cold gut check and ask myself what *I* think I should do, I just don't know. It kills me, because I've always known, on that deep-down level, what to do in any situation—even when the answer isn't particularly pleasant.

Since I can't concentrate on my homework, I go to my computer and sign on to my e-mail, since it's my fave form of procrastination. As I type in my password, though, I realize that I could have a reply from Sean. If so, I'm going to have to deal with it. Somehow.

So much for relaxing procrastination.

Then it hits me that the funniest—and most pathetic—part of all is that whenever I've had trouble with any of my girlfriends, I've always called Sean to talk it through. For a long time, it's been either Sean or Dad, since I don't have a mom around the house

like my friends do. And Sean was always
really good at looking at things objectively
and giving me advice about how to handle
things. He was usually dead-on, too.

Funny, the things I miss about him.

To: TnnsGrl@VVHSnet.edu
From: SeanNorx@freedommail.ct.com
Subject: Us

<<But in the long run, I realize that you
were right. I don't know how
anyone—even people as into each other as
we've been the past couple years—can sustain a relationship from all the way
across the country.>>

Chloe,
  Here's the thing: I don't know if I
really was right. That's part of why I e-
mailed you in the first place.
  I guess what I'm saying is that I miss you
like crazy. I know we're long
distance, and I know I've probably messed this
up beyond repair, but would you think about us
trying to do this? If anyone can make this
work, I think we can.

Let me know if you'll be around Saturday
night—I'm not doing anything, so maybe I
can call and we can have a talk and figure
out if it's worth a shot.
Love,
Sean

To: SeanNorx@freedommail.ct.com
From: TnnsGrl@VVHSnet.edu
Subject: RE: Us

Sean,
   Well . . . WOW. I'm not really sure what
to say. I'm actually out on Saturday
night, but maybe we can talk on Sunday, if
you're around. Let me know?
Always,
Chloe

Six

Almost there, almost there, almost there. My brain pounds out the words with every slap of my Asics against the packed dirt on the cross-country trail. It's a three-way meet—Vista Verde High School, Boulder High School, and Golden High School—and the cross-country trail is crowded with hard-core runners, breathing hard and elbowing one another if necessary to pass. Needless to say, no one's stopping to pee in the woods.

At least this first meet's at home. I'd be ten times more nervous if we were running on an unfamiliar route.

And, of course, I have the e-mail from Sean to distract my brain from the fact that

I'm in the middle of a *race*, not to mention the whole Rachel-Billy thing—which really is the bigger issue. Kendra bugged me all day yesterday about telling Rachel, but since I didn't even see Rachel—she had a dentist appointment during lunch—I couldn't have talked to her if I'd wanted to.

Part of me is relieved I didn't get the chance, but part of me feels like it's this weight hanging over my head, getting ready to drop and crush my skull. And since tonight's poker at Billy's, I need to come up with a way to deal with this ASAP.

The voices I've been hearing in front of me, from the direction of the school, suddenly get a lot louder, meaning the first of the guys are about to finish the course.

Almost there, almost there. I summon up what little oomph I have left and kick hard so I can pass two girls from Golden High School just before we leave the wooded trail for the last stretch of path, the part leading to the track and the finish line.

Football's away this weekend—they're playing in Arvada, I think—and the girls' softball team isn't taking the field for about an hour. Given that timing, I assumed there was no way anyone would show up for cross-country. But no, the stands near the track are packed.

Crowds. Lots of people *watching* me. Just what I need.

I pass a tall, dark-haired girl from Boulder, but I can feel her right on my shoulder, running hard, as the crowd starts yelling in front of us.

Where did all these people come from? Who gets their jollies from watching people *run*? This can't possibly be the way it is all season. Maybe it's just a first-sporting-event-of-the-year thing.

Oh man, my legs are going to fall off. It's like I'm losing muscle control over them. I vaguely wonder if people ever pass out or hurl as they run the last tenth of a mile.

I hit the track with the girl from Boulder right next to me. I run as hard as I can, but my knees want to buckle in opposite directions. I manage to give an extra hard couple of kicks as I round the last corner, and I hear the girl from Boulder grunt to keep up.

Then I beat her across the finish line.

I run a few more ragged steps, then totter off to the inside of the track and collapse in the grass next to a few other runners. The girl from Boulder stands in the grass near me, taking deep breaths, her hands folded together on top of her head. "Good run," she says, then grins at me.

"You too," I tell her, doing my best to smile back. "I'd have sworn you had it."

"Wasn't expecting you to come flying out of the woods like that." She extends a hand, helping me up to a more respectable standing position. "I'll be ready for you next time," she says, and we both laugh, even though it comes out like we're both delirious from lack of oxygen.

The Boulder coach walks over and hands the girl a paper cup with water. "How're you doing, Chantelle?"

"Fine," she manages between slurps.

"Fifth place today. Great effort," he says, then moves on to talk to a knot of three of the guys who finished not too far ahead of me and Chantelle.

Of course, all I can think is that I came in fourth. *Fourth!* Out of three teams of high school girls!

I tell Chantelle it was nice to meet her, then wander toward the stands to find Dad, since he has my water bottle. Within seconds, I spot him at end of the bleachers and head his way, hoping I'm not walking funny since my legs are wobbly and I'm suddenly feeling light-headed. He's grinning ear to ear as he holds out the bottle. "Chloe, that was fantastic!"

"Peachy, Dad. Just great. Now I think I'm going to die," I say, then grab for the bottle. As people from the stands glance over at us, I realize how red my face must be and how sweaty and gross I probably look. I try to focus on my dad once I'm done slugging back all the water I can handle. "I think my legs are going to fall off. No kidding."

"You did look a little rubbery coming around the track at the end. I'm amazed you held her off like that. That took a lot of determination." He puts his arm around my shoulders—apparently oblivious to the fact that I'm sweating like a wrestler fresh from the weight room—and gives me a squeeze.

I want to shrug out from under his arm,

just because of the nasty factor, but I stay put since he doesn't seem to mind. And I love that he thinks I have determination. No one's told me I have determination before. Ever.

"You going to come home with me, or ride with your friends?"

I'm beat, and it feels so good just to walk next to Dad and suck down water, but I promised Amy I'd stick around to see her game. "My stuff's in the locker room. I think I'll take a shower and watch Amy's game. Can I meet you at home for lunch?"

"Fine by me." He gives me a final shoulder squish, then lets go. As he fishes his car keys out of his front pocket, he says, "I'm really proud of you, Chloe. Not because you did so well—which is great—but because you're trying so hard. You're seeing what you're capable of doing."

I can tell he's getting emotional, which is so not Dad. He knows it too, because of course right then he offers to take in any dry cleaning I have since he's heading to the Clean & Brite pretty soon with all his suits.

"Nah, I'm good," I say, just as I hear

someone walking up behind me. Dad nods at whoever it is, tells me he'll catch me at home, then turns and heads toward the parking lot.

"Did I interrupt?" Eric asks.

"Nope, my dad was just checking on my plans." His face is a little red, but he doesn't seem too wiped out. I gesture toward the track. "How'd you do?"

"Sixth for the guys," he says. "But I saw your finish. That rocked! Fourth for the girls and sixteenth overall. Way to go!"

I can't help it. I feel a huge, dopey grin spread across my face. He cracks up, then grabs me and spins me around in a big hug, which cracks me up in return.

"You didn't think I had it in me, did you?" Before he can say anything, I lean on his shoulder and fake like I'm going to collapse—which I still might anyway. Good thing he has pretty strong shoulders. "I think I'm going to have a heart attack right here."

"You're gonna give me a heart attack."

I straighten up and smile at him. "Honestly? I didn't think I was going to make it without falling at the end."

"Next practice, try going into overdrive at the end, just like you did today. Imagine there's someone going neck and neck with you. You'll start to figure out how to get past the jelly legs. I bet that was it, huh? Jelly legs at the end?"

"Total jelly legs."

Eric nods toward the finish line, where the last of the runners are coming in. "Coach'll probably want to say something to the team before we can go. Come on."

He starts toward Coach McCarthy, and I try to discreetly wipe my face on my shirt as I follow him toward the field, scanning the stands as I walk. I spy Kendra and Rachel sitting near the top and raise my hand to catch their attention, but they're talking to Alyssa and a couple other girls we've known forever, so they don't see me wave to them. Then, off to the far side of the bleachers, wearing her softball uniform, I see Amy. She has her glove tucked under one arm and her duffel bag slung over her other shoulder. I wave to her, and she gives me a thumbs-up sign, then claps and does a very fake, over-the-top cheer. I shake my head at her craziness, even though I'm really glad she was able to see me run, since she got me into it in the first place. I gesture toward the softball field to let her know I'll come watch her when I'm done. She gives me the okay sign, then cuts back behind the bleachers, toward the parking lot, I assume to go to the locker room.

I take a couple jogging steps to catch up to Eric, but something makes me glance over my shoulder toward Amy.

She's a good distance away, crossing the parking lot, but she's walking very fast, like she's angry all of a sudden. I stop to watch her, trying to see if there's someone following her.

Then I see her wipe the side of her face as if she's trying to get rid of tears. She opens the back door to the gym, flinging it hard before going inside.

What the hell?

I glance back toward the stands. Rachel and Kendra are still talking to Alyssa, and I wonder if they got into it with Amy over something. She's usually able to blow them off whenever they argue about stuff, though.

"Chloe?"

"Yeah?" I turn toward Eric.

"What's up?" He looks in the direction I was just looking and frowns. "Was that Amy?"

"Huh? Um, yeah, I think so. It's about time for her to get geared up for softball." I play dumb. I figure she'll want her privacy, whatever it is that pissed her off. I grab Eric's arm and steer him back toward the finish line. "Let's go listen to Coach McCarthy."

"Full house, sixes over kings." Billy spreads his cards on the table, then shoots his sister, Fiona, a look of sibling superiority before swooping up the pile of chips in the middle of the table.

"You've gotten much better at bluffing," Fiona says. "I was planning on coming home and cleaning you out. You're screwing up all my plans."

She's smiling as she says this, though. We've been sitting at a table in their basement rec room for about an hour—me, Billy, Fiona and her boyfriend, Zach, and her roommate, Emily—and I've decided already that I really like her. She's very relaxed and Zen-like. Kind of the way I see Kendra being when she goes to college.

Okay, I cannot think about Kendra. Or the fact that I didn't get to talk to Rachel this afternoon like Kendra wanted. I expected them to come over to Amy's softball game, so I mentally rehearsed about a dozen ways to tell Rachel about my not-a-date with Billy, but they apparently arrived and left while I was still in the locker room. I probably could have called her, but it just didn't seem like a phone kind of thing.

As Zach starts to deal the next hand, I ask Fiona how she likes CSU, just to distract myself.

"Love it," she says. "Made the mistake of staying in the dorms for my sophomore year, though, trying to save money. Next year, Em and I are definitely getting an apartment off-campus. We're the only sophomores on our floor."

Emily makes a little noise of agreement as she takes two cards from the dealer, then she asks me about my college plans.

"Well, I'm just a junior now. But I'm leaning toward Colorado State. Depends on whether I get any scholarship money from CU, though. Between the two schools, I may end up going wherever it's cheaper for me."

"That's what I did," Zach says. "Picked CSU because I had more scholarship money there. But I lucked out. Turned out CSU is way better than CU." He shoots a look at Fiona, then adds, "Better women."

"Yep, that's the criteria to use," Billy says as he folds. I look at my hand and do the same. My cards are worthless tonight. We're playing for pretty low stakes, but I'm already down fifteen bucks. Billy, on the other hand, is cleaning up. So is Emily. In the end, I think the two of them are going to wipe out the rest of us.

"You'll fit right in at CSU," Zach says. "Billy told Fi that you're really smart. He neglected to mention the pretty part, though."

Fiona elbows him, but not in a mean way. "Yeah. My dear, ultrabrain brother didn't tell us you're gorgeous." She winks at Billy. "We wouldn't have believed him, anyway."

"Thanks," Billy mutters. It's clear she's teasing him, and that this isn't a big thing, but I still feel uncomfortable. Someday I'll figure out how to handle compliments on my looks without getting all tense. I need to be the way Billy is when his sister calls him a geek.

When the hand is over, Zach calls for a bathroom break and runs upstairs. Emily immediately whips out her cell phone to check in with her boyfriend, who stayed in Fort Collins for the weekend to cram for an exam he has on Monday.

Fiona puts her chips in neat little stacks, then follows Zach upstairs, hollering down to us that she's going up to the second-floor bathroom since Zach already grabbed the one on the first floor. Of course, she adds some pointed comments about how he should have been a gentleman and left the downstairs one for the women.

Billy nods toward the stairs. "Come on. We can grab more Cokes for everyone and refill the popcorn bowl."

Since I'm just as happy to give Emily some privacy, I follow him out of the basement and into the kitchen. He grabs a bag of popcorn from a cupboard, then sticks it in the microwave while I look out the row of windows at the rear of the kitchen.

I'm about to tell him how beautiful it is, since his house is in the foothills and I can see the lights of Denver glittering off in the distance, over the tops of the pine trees, but Zach comes in and starts rifling through the fridge, looking for a beer to take downstairs.

I don't think he's of age, but since I'm not certain, I don't say anything. Billy and Fiona didn't say anything about the fact that he'd had a beer earlier, so I figure it's no big deal.

He finds an opener and flips off the top, then says, "Oh, Fi and I invited my cousin and some other friends over. They'll probably be here in an hour or so. I think they were going to the movies first. We should be able to finish up the poker game before they get here. You guys are welcome to stay if you want. Or take off if you want. Whatever. We're just gonna hang out and watch the football game. CSU's playing Wyoming tonight."

"Yeah, Fi mentioned that," Billy says. "No problem by me."

"Me either," I say. Zach grins, then heads upstairs to find Fiona.

The popcorn's still got a couple minutes to go, so I turn back to the windows. "This is really pretty, Billy."

"Yeah, I like this house," he says. Even though it's fairly dark—just the light from the microwave and the light from the staircase down to the basement are coming in— I can tell he's smiling. "It's peaceful."

"And you can't beat the view."

"You should see it during the day. From the family room, we can see all the way across to the Flatirons. We get foxes in the backyard sometimes too."

"My dad and I are in the older part of Vista Verde," I tell him. "A little farther downhill. Our view isn't this good. But we get a fox every once in a while. I know most people hate them, but I don't at all."

I can feel him moving in closer behind me, looking over my shoulder, out at the city lights. "Me too. Freaks Fi out when one pounces on a mouse or a gopher and kills it, though."

"Yeah, I try not to think about that part."

The smell of popcorn fills the kitchen. A couple seconds later, the microwave starts to beep.

"Thirty seconds," Billy says. He leans forward, putting his hands on the windowsill. We're quiet for a few heartbeats, just looking out at the lights together. I can feel the connection between us, like we had that first day in independent study when we smiled at each other, and I wonder if he's feeling it too.

Finally, he says, "I'm glad you came, Chloe. I know it's probably not as exciting as your usual Saturday night, but I'm having fun."

"Me too. I really like seeing you away from school and all the commotion there." And I mean it. It's new and different being with him here, away from everyone and everything.

And I like that Billy is so protective of me. Not in a superior way, but in a polite way—making sure I'm comfortable, offering me a drink, and just generally checking to make sure I'm having a good time, even though he really doesn't have to.

I run a hand over the windowsill. Most

kids I know throw parties when their parents are out. Billy and his sister seem a lot more respectful of their parents' house—taking care not to make a mess of it—the same way I treat the house I share with Dad. It's just a more grown-up attitude, I guess. One I don't see too often around school.

"Exactly," he says. "Oh, and I didn't want to say anything downstairs, 'cause I was afraid you might get embarrassed, but you kicked ass at cross-country today. I'm impressed."

I turn toward him. The moonlight reflects off his glasses, making it difficult to interpret his expression. "How'd you know about that?"

"I was there."

"You were?"

I can feel his smile in the semidark almost as well as I can see it. "Yep. I had the day shift at WooWoo, but I stopped by the school beforehand. Saw you right at the finish line. Sorry I couldn't stick around, though."

"No, that's okay. Thanks for coming." I'm totally self-conscious about it now, though. I probably looked awful. And even though I'm glad I finished as well as I did, I don't think I lived up to my Super Runner secret identity doing it. I was more like a stumbling, dying runner.

"Wouldn't have missed it."

And then he's leaning in, so close that I can feel his breath on my face. I can tell he's trying to work up the courage to kiss me and he's just about done it.

And I don't know if I should let him kiss me or not. I want to, but bad. I'm dying to know if he's any good. And how the whole kissing-with-glasses thing would work. But it feels wrong if I haven't gotten the go-ahead from Rachel.

Then the microwave beeps, letting us know the popcorn's done. I'm sure that's the end of it, that the spell between us is broken, but he doesn't move. "Chloe," his voice is barely audible. "Is it okay if—"

"It's okay."

And then he's kissing me. Gently, like I haven't been kissed in a long time. And it's so different from Sean. Billy feels different, smells different. And he's a little taller, too, which I hadn't even realized until now. One of his hands comes up by my cheek, his fingers sliding so they just start to tangle in my hair. His mouth is warm and sweet, and he knows just what to do.

And my legs are getting that jelly feeling again.

I can hear Fiona and Zach laughing about something upstairs, then the microwave lets out a warning beep to remind us to get the popcorn.

"You sure you don't mind?" His mouth is close to my ear, and the skin of his cheek brushing against mine as he asks the question feels so, so right.

I should tell him to stop. I *know* I should. But standing here in the kitchen, with the smell of popcorn filling the air and Billy's chest just grazing mine, with the twinkling lights and pine trees just outside, it feels like Rachel's a million miles away.

"I don't mind." I'm dying inside, as a matter of fact.

He kisses me again, and it's perfect. Like we're trying this out, seeing what we think of each other, with no commitment but an awful lot of promise. I wrap my arms around his waist, letting my fingers wander across the back of his shirt, right where it meets his jeans. I want to slide my hands up, move his shirt out of the way. Feel the muscles of his back. The warmth of his skin.

I pull him a fraction of an inch closer and let him deepen the kiss.

Wow, but he is *good*. Holy smokin'—

"Hey, you guys making more popcorn?" Fiona yells from the second floor. "I can smell it!"

Billy pulls back, though his fingers are still playing with my hair. "Yeah," he calls out. "It's almost done."

"'Kay," Fiona yells back. "We'll be down in a sec."

Billy leans in for another kiss even as he eases his hand away from my cheek. I can feel his smile against my lips, and it makes me smile back. "Guess we're about to be interrupted."

"Probably," I whisper, dropping my hands from his waist. I'll figure out what to do about Rachel later. I should be able to have both my friends and this whatever-it-is that's starting between Billy and me.

He walks over to the microwave and pops the door open, then grabs an oversize bowl from one of the cabinets and pours the popcorn into it. As he pours, he leans over and gives me a long, soft kiss on my temple. Like he couldn't resist getting in one more before we head downstairs to finish playing poker.

I smile up at him and, as I catch his eye, it occurs to me that I didn't even notice his glasses while we were kissing.

Cool.

"Whaddya mean you're on Ridgeback Road?" I hear Zach's voice coming from the stairs and the pounding of his feet on the treads, heading our way and severing the connection between Billy and me. A moment later, he and Fiona come into the kitchen. "What happened to the movie? Okay, okay. It's number—hey, Fi, this is 22 Ridgeback, right?"

Fiona nods, and Zach relays it to whoever's on the other end of the cell phone and tells them to look for his car in the driveway, then hangs up.

"I take it we're not finishing the poker game?" Billy asks as Zach and Fiona turn toward the living room, where the floor-to-ceiling windows face the street.

"Movie was sold out, sounds like."

Billy picks up the popcorn bowl, gives me a look that says, *What can we do?* and we follow them out to the living room. Zach's taking long sips on his bottle of Coors as he stares out the window closest to the front door. "They're at the bottom of the hill," he says between drinks, "so they should be pulling up . . . yep, there they are."

A pair of headlights appears, then swings into the driveway. At the same time, Emily comes up from the basement. "They're here?" she asks. "Well, guess we can turn on the pregame coverage and start early."

Fiona agrees, then turns back toward the kitchen and flips on all the lights. I ask if there's anything I can do to help and I end up fishing Cokes out of the fridge and carrying them out to the living room. We set them on the coffee table, next to where Billy's already put the popcorn. Fiona follows behind me with a bowl full of pretzels.

Zach opens the door and waves everyone in. A couple guys come in and knock fists with Zach. They're clearly friends of his from CSU, since they seem to know Emily and Fiona, too. Then Fort Collins Pete from school comes in. Zach starts to make introductions, saying that Pete's his cousin, but Billy and Pete largely ignore him and wave to each other in acknowledgment—one of those "I know you from school, don't I?" kind of things.

Me, I just freeze.

If Pete's here, I know who I must be hearing coming up the walk behind him.

Sure enough, a very familiar female laugh erupts right near the door, then Rachel comes in. She's attached at the hip to Gorgeous Jake, the senior, even as she leans forward and says something funny to Pete that makes it clear she's leaving her options open. Then she looks up and catches my eye. A grin splits her face ear to ear. "Chloe! What are you doing here?"

Before I can answer her question, though, her eyes dart behind me and a look of suspicion crosses her face. She tries to cover the suspicious part with a forced smile, but I know better when she says, "And Billy! You're here too?"

"I live here," Billy says, laughing at Rachel's confusion. He obviously has no freaking clue that Rachel's into him, or he wouldn't be giving her such a warm greeting after he spent the last couple minutes kissing me.

The cesspool into which I've stepped is getting deeper by the second.

"Billy invited me to come over and play poker with his sister and her friends," I tell Rachel, trying to make it clear that this was—at least originally—a totally casual thing. "But I'm getting cleaned out. And Zach"—I point to where Zach and Pete are talking—"he's Pete's cousin and Billy's sister's boyfriend. Isn't that cool?" I'm saying it like I'm hinting to her that is her "in" to get to know Fort Collins Pete even better. Or something.

I don't even know what I'm doing, at this point. Desperately trying to cover my tail, I suppose.

"Did you know I was coming over here?" Rachel asks, pulling me a few steps away from everyone else so we can talk quietly without being obvious. I force myself not to look at Billy, who's now talking to

Fiona, just because I don't want Rachel to read anything into it.

"No, no idea. I'm glad you did, though." I say this with a huge smile, pretending I never saw that distrustful look on her face when she saw me and Billy together. "I was trying to find you and Kendra at Amy's softball game this afternoon so I could tell you about Billy inviting me over. Where'd you two go?"

"I went to get a manicure. Wanted to look good for tonight." She holds up her hand and wiggles her fingers, which are a soft pink that perfectly matches her sleeveless top. "Kendra decided to tag along and get a manicure too."

"Oh."

I'm trying to figure out how to ask her about Amy—if they had an argument or something before the game—partially because I'm curious, and partially to distract her from thinking about me being here with Billy, when she cuts me off. "Um, so when did Billy ask you to come over for poker? This morning? I saw him hanging around near the bleachers at cross-country."

Oh, man. "Um, no, it was during independent study on Thursday. I didn't get the chance to tell you—"

"Thursday? Then why didn't you say something at WooWoo?" She pauses, looks past me toward where Billy is talking to Jake and Pete, then frowns and says, "Is there something going on between you guys? Something you're not telling me?"

I can't lie and say no. But I can't lie and say yes, either. Now I really wish I'd told her earlier—before Billy kissed me. "Honestly? I don't know. That's why I wanted to talk to you. To see what you thought first."

Her eyes widen. "Oh. My. God. I cannot believe you!"

"What?"

She just rolls her eyes and lets out a laugh that's more of a cackle, which draws a couple of looks from the guys. From Rachel's expression and tone of voice, I can't gauge if she's mad or surprised or what.

"What?" I ask, trying to keep my voice low. "Tell me."

"It's nothing," she says aloud. "Absolutely

nothing." She brushes by me and takes a few steps to stand between Jake and Pete, somehow managing to flirt with both of them and with Billy at the same time.

I walk over to the sofa near where they're standing, sit down, grab a Diet Coke from the coffee table, and try to tell myself that Rachel gets mad fast and gets over it fast, just like Amy does. And if I talk to her later, when no one else is around, I can clear this up before it becomes A Thing.

And maybe I'll luck out and she'll hook up with either Gorgeous Jake or Fort Collins Pete, and my whole maybe-this-is-something with Billy won't matter. I pop the top on my soda, but before I even have the first sip, Billy's sitting beside me.

So *not* what I need with Rachel being the way she's being—which is constantly looking over at me, even while she's giggling (and I do mean giggling) at everything Jake or Pete say.

"Sorry 'bout not finishing the poker game," Billy says as he scoops up a handful of popcorn, oblivious to Rachel. "I didn't think they'd be here for a while."

"No problem. I was only going to lose more money."

"Still." He lets the word hang, and I can tell he's thinking what I am. That we liked being away from everyone we know at school, if only for a little while.

And I can tell he's thinking about our kiss, too. In a good way.

He pours half his handful of popcorn into my hand, then grins at me. "Maybe we can plan something for next weekend, if you're not too busy with the popular crowd."

"Or if you're not busy with the Dungeons & Dragons crowd," I tease back.

His fingers brush against mine. Instantly, I look up to see if Rachel's looking at us.

Naturally, she is. She avoids my gaze, instead turning back toward Fort Collins Pete.

"I hate to ditch, but I should probably head home," I tell him. "I'm more wiped out from cross-country today than I thought. You don't mind, do you?"

"Nah." He's totally cool about it, and my respect for him goes up one more notch for not reading the slightest thing into my wanting to go. Sean would've argued with me, wanting me to stay. "Want me to walk you to your car?"

"I'm good. Stay and be entertaining." No way do I want Rachel to see him walk outside with me. I ask him to tell Fiona that I appreciated being part of the poker game and meeting her boyfriend and roommate, then duck out the front door. It's one of those warm September nights where you don't need a jacket, even though you can tell ski season is right around the corner.

I take a deep breath, slide into my car and start it up, and hope like mad that Rachel's still speaking to me tomorrow. If she is, then I know we'll work it all out.

Someone pounds on my car window, about sending my heart rate into the stratosphere. "Hey. It's Chloe, right?"

I look over to see Gorgeous Jake's face staring in my window. I hit the button on my armrest to roll down the window and say hey.

"You're a friend of Rachel's, right? I've seen you around school."

I smile. Good. Maybe he wants to talk

to me about her. "Yeah. Rachel's great, isn't she?"

"Yeah, she is." He leans forward, resting his hands where they'll get eaten by my window if I push the button again. He pauses for a sec, then says, "Look, I'm not sure where you live, so maybe it's out of your way, but would you mind giving me a ride home?"

Whoa. I ask where he lives. It's only a couple miles from my house, so I tell him to hop in. I barely know the guy, but he has a decent enough reputation that I figure he's safe. As soon as he's buckled in and I'm heading downhill, thinking how I can make this work for Rachel—and save my own tail from her wrath in the process—he says, "It's cool I ran into you back there. I've heard lots about you."

Is he kidding me? "Really?"

"Well, you're kind of hard to miss, you know? You're not exactly the ugliest girl in school."

I give the casual laugh I always do when I get this type of comment, then try to change the subject. "Um, hey, do I make a right or a left up here?"

"Left. Anyway, I was wondering . . ." Oh, no. I know what's coming. And I think I'm going to die, especially since he's shifting in his seat so his hand is only a few inches from where I stupidly have mine resting on the emergency brake separating us. "Would you be interested in going out sometime? Just coffee or whatever?"

"Casual?"

"Not necessarily. But sure, if you want it to be."

I mentally utter a variation of "oh, shit" that would not only shock Amy, it'd have her giving me a 9.8 for creativity. "Well, I'm not sure."

I should just tell him to blow, but I can't. Wouldn't that be rude? I'm so used to using the "I have a boyfriend" excuse (which wasn't really an excuse—it was true) that I don't have a clue how to turn a guy down without hurting his feelings.

He actually has the guts—or maybe the ego—to laugh at me. "You allergic to caffeine?"

"No," I say, then give a very pointed look at the day-old takeout of Seattle's Best that's sitting in my cup holder. "It's"—I go for the old excuse—"I'm kind of seeing someone."

If Billy kissed me, that counts, right?

"Oh, sorry." He doesn't seem the least bit bothered. "I heard you and Sean Norcross were going out. But I thought you broke up. My bad."

"No, it's okay." I'm tempted to tell him it's not Sean, but figure the less said, the better.

"Turn right here, then left at the first stop sign. I'm the last house on the left."

I make two quick turns, then pull into the driveway in front of an older home that's clearly been redone. Even in the dark, I can tell that landscapers have been here.

"Thanks," he says, giving my arm a squeeze just above my elbow. "And if you're ever not sort of seeing someone, see me."

I give him a friendly wave as he closes the car door, then back out without checking to see if he goes in the house. I pull back out onto the main road, but instead of going home, I make an impulse turn into the McDonald's drive-thru. I need some real food since I missed out on the football game appetizers. I hand my money to the girl at the window, then start fiddling with the radio. While I'm waiting for my food, though, the stoplight at the corner changes and a little red pickup screeches to a stop, catching my attention.

And damned if it's not Gorgeous Jake at the wheel. The light turns, and he barrels through, heading back along the road we'd just driven.

When I get my food—after a long wait—I can't help it. I drive back to Billy's. Sure enough, Jake's red pickup is parked in the street at the end of the driveway.

I buzz past and head for home.

At the end of the night, when everyone leaves, I wonder how he's going to explain his truck.

I wonder what Rachel will think.

I wonder what Billy will think.

Seven

"Chloe! You!"

I blink up at the ceiling of my still-dark room, confused. I don't hear anything but the soft whir of my bedroom fan, so I roll back over.

"Chloe Elizabeth Rand! Telephone!"

Is he kidding? I didn't hear it ring. And hello?! It's *dark*.

Shaking myself to something passing for alertness, I grab for the phone, yelling back to Dad that I've got it once I manage to pick up.

According to the dial on my vintage Hello Kitty bedside clock, it's only six in the morning. Who calls at this hour? Who even calls three hours *after* this hour? Anyone who knows me knows I like to sleep in on the weekends for as long as Dad will let me. Whatever it is, it must be important.

And even though my brain's foggy—I think I must've been in the middle of a dream—I can guess who it is.

"Hello?" I say, hoping I sound clearer—and less guilty—than I feel.

"Hello yourself, beautiful one."

"Um, hey." My voice comes out sounding harsh, but I was expecting to hear Rachel, and this is most definitely not Rachel. "Sean?"

"Sorry 'bout the time. I know it's really early, but my parents want to take me shopping for more stuff for our new house, and since we're two hours ahead of you—"

"No, no, it's okay." How could I have spaced that I told him it'd be cool if he wanted to call today? And why did I do that again?

"It's good to hear your voice."

I push up on my elbow, then slide my rear end toward my headboard so I'm upright. "It's good to hear yours, too, Sean."

I probably shouldn't admit it, but it is, despite the fact that I'm fighting not to yawn into the phone. Amy's my best friend, but in many ways, for the last two years Sean has been too. There's a comfort level in hearing him first thing in the morning, even though I know this call won't be what he's hoping for.

He tells me a little about his school in Connecticut and the new house he and his family have moved into, and I tell him about what's going on at school and how I did yesterday at cross-country. He makes a couple jokes about me scoring points at a track meet for the Vista Verde Vermin before telling me that he managed to make the football team at his new school. Then he gets quiet for a second, which I know means the nicey-nice small talk part of our conversation is over. "It sounds like you're doing pretty well," he finishes. "Are you really?"

"Yeah, so far," I answer, even though I know what he wants to know—and it has nothing to do with school or sports.

I'm too wiped out to have this conversation. I need to think about what I should say instead of shooting from the hip, but short of faking a sudden need to go talk to my dad about something, I can't figure a way out. Besides, he'd hear it in my voice and *know* I was faking.

"Do you miss me, Chloe?" He doesn't sound pathetic or needy at all. Just very matter-of-fact, let's-figure-out-if-we-have-a-shot about the whole thing.

"Of course I do," I say. "We were together for a long time. But . . . well, I can't lie to you, Sean, so—"

"I'd know if you were lying."

"True." I swear our brains are still connected somehow. Maybe that's why he's making this easier than I expected. "I wouldn't want to lie to you anyway."

"Good. So tell me straight out."

"Well . . ." *Here goes.* I close my eyes and say, "The thing is, I think our breaking up has actually been good for me. If you'd been here this year, I would have planned my whole junior year around you. And my whole senior year after that. But I've been forced to step back and think about what I really want."

It's quiet on the other end of the line. I

open my eyes and stare at the wall, waiting for him to say something. Hopefully something positive.

"And what you really want isn't me?" Again, he doesn't sound whiny, just thoughtful. His usual matter-of-fact Sean self.

"It was. But it isn't right now. Somewhere along the line, I stopped being Chloe Rand, who just happened to be going out with Sean Norcross, and started being half of Chloe and Sean. It wasn't that I made a mistake going out with you—it's more that I let it take over who I was. If that makes any sense at all."

And if it doesn't, well, I don't have any other explanation.

I hear a long, slow exhale from his end of the line. It's a little tic of his when he's trying to stay unemotional without anyone knowing it. "So I assume this means you don't want to try again?"

I can feel his heart breaking across the phone line, despite his steady voice and laid-back attitude. And even though he stomped on my heart and left it for dead, I know that deep down he really does regret doing it.

"I think it's better this way," I finally say, even though I hate making him feel the same way he made me feel. "But maybe this can be good for both of us. It'll give us a chance to make new friends—especially you, since you're in a new town and everything. You know, I realized during the first week of school when you weren't here that I hadn't made a new friend since we started going out? I never cared about meeting anyone new or getting to know anyone else."

"But you're meeting new people now?"

"Yeah, I am." The instant I say it, I wish I hadn't. He's going to think this is about another guy or something.

Instantly, I picture kissing Billy last night and feel horribly, terribly guilty. I know I shouldn't, but I do. Mostly because kissing Billy felt so wonderful and romantic and *right*. Like maybe it's what I've been waiting for all along.

"Or maybe it's that you're getting to know old friends better without me around?"

I frown and lean back into my pillows. The way he said it, it's obvious it wasn't a casual comment about me spending more time with Amy or my other girlfriends now that I'm not part of a couple. "What do you mean?"

"I think you know what I mean. But it's okay with me. Guess I should have known it'd happen."

"Known *what*?"

"The whole cross-country thing. I know all about it. I just didn't think it could be serious. But it's really all right—maybe it'll even be good for you. Just don't kid yourself and think that you're all independent and everything, okay?"

My brain must really still be sleep-addled. "Sean, I don't know what you're talking about."

"Never mind, then." He lets out an exasperated breath. "If we can't be together, I s'pose we can still be friends, right? I know that's clichéd and everything, but we know each other better than anyone does. No reason we can't be civil and e-mail now and then and keep up. You think?"

"I'd like that," I tell him. "And you never know. Maybe we'll still end up at the same college. Like we'd always thought. It'd be nice to be friends."

He laughs, and the sound of it makes me feel comfortable again. "Yeah, you never know. Hey, my parents are hollering. Time to go shopping. But e-mail me and let me know what's going on with you when you're comfortable talking about it. The real scoop, okay? I know I was a real jackass at DIA, but I want you to be happy—though I wish it wasn't with another guy."

"Yeah, okay." I tell him to have fun shopping, then hang up, more confused than before he called.

I snuggle back into bed and pull the sheets right up to my neck so I'm back in the same position as when Dad started yelling. I can't get back to sleep, though. I keep replaying what Sean was saying at the end of our call—all that meeting new people and me not being as independent as I think stuff—and it just doesn't make sense. He never met Billy except in passing at WooWoo, so he wouldn't think me hooking up with Billy would be "getting to know old friends better"—assuming he knew something about Billy, which he couldn't possibly know unless Rachel e-mailed him in the last five or six hours with her suspicions.

And suspicions is all they could be, even then.

So what the hell? Especially with the cross-country talk . . .

Then it hits me that maybe he thinks I went out for cross-country to meet guys. Since he's always told me—from the time we started going out—that I could get any guy I wanted (not that *I* believe that, but I really think he did, and probably still does), maybe he thinks I've hooked up with someone on the team.

Great.

I roll over, pissed off that he'd think I'd do that—just go trolling for guys like Rachel does. Not that there's anything wrong with Rachel's trolling. I actually admire that she has such a strong will to go out and get exactly what she wants. It's just that it's not *me*, and Sean of all people should know that.

"Probably the only reason he wanted to get back together," I mutter into my pillow. Jealousy, pure and simple. I'll have to tell Rachel, Kendra, and Amy. Maybe they'll finally realize I was right not to go crawling back to Sean when I got that first e-mail from him.

"Chloe, I'm leaving!"

"Okay! Feel free to leave your ammo behind!" I holler back, just as happy to have the house to myself, knowing he'll lock up on his way out to meet his hunting buddies and leave me to snooze as long as I like.

I try to go back to sleep since this is a rare opportunity, but now that my brain is engaged it's just not happening. Too many thoughts of Billy and Rachel and Gorgeous Jake and the whole conversation with Sean.

I really want to call Rachel, but I'm positive she's even more dead to the world than I was when Sean called. It's not even six thirty yet, according to Hello Kitty.

So I do the unthinkable. I click on my bedside lamp, pull out the book we're supposed to read next in honors English, and actually start.

On the third ring, someone finally picks up the phone.

"Hi, Mrs. Nielsen," I say, recognizing her voice. It's very mom-ish, the kind that always makes you think she's about to invite you over for brownies and milk and ask after your family's health. "It's Chloe. Rachel there?"

"I'm sorry, sweetheart, she's not. Her father drove her to go book shopping with Amy. I think they were going to stop at Barnes & Noble first, and then drive into Denver to look at The Tattered Cover. I just got home myself, so I'm haven't heard from them about when they'll be back. Maybe you can try her cell?"

"Okay, thanks, Mrs. Nielsen. I'll do that." Of course, I've already done that. It rang and rang, then went to voice mail. Since Rachel has her ringer on whenever she's not in class or at a movie, I know she's just ignoring me.

And apparently, she's ignoring me with Amy. If she's pouring her guts out to Amy about seeing me at Billy's, I sure hope Amy's setting her straight.

I try Amy's cell, but it goes into voice mail on the first ring, which means she probably didn't bother taking it with her, which is pretty typical Amy. She tends to forget it in her bedroom charger.

Since Dad's out shooting at poor, defenseless waterfowl (which I will not, not, not think about), I go crash in the family room, click on the TV, and flip channels until I find a mindless entertainment report. After a half hour of listening to speculation about some sitcom actress's exercise routine and an overly detailed discussion of a British rock star's latest charity trip to Southeast Asia, I start writing up my chemistry lab, since it's due tomorrow.

It's the ultimate boring Sunday. In other words, there's nothing to distract me from thinking about Rachel. Or Billy. Or Rachel and Billy and what I did or didn't do wrong.

Finally, I pick up the phone and try Kendra. I hate doing the girly drama bit, but I really need to know if Rachel's pissed off, just taking this all in stride, or what.

Kendra's dad picks up. She's at her church youth group car wash—which I forgot about—and won't be home until late because there's apparently a pizza outing afterward.

Strike three for Chloe. No Rachel, no Amy, and now no Kendra.

I leave a message for her to call me if she gets home before nine, then spend the afternoon curled up in my bed reading Steinbeck. Not sure I absorb much of it, though. I keep having to go back to reread paragraphs because I lose track of the time line and who did what to whom. All I know is, Steinbeck writes about some pretty messed-up people.

At ten o'clock, I give up. Other than a four thirty call from Dad to tell me he's bringing home dinner (thankfully from a restaurant, and not in the form of an animal whose life he abruptly ended), the phone doesn't ring once.

"Hey, looked for you at the lockers," I say to Amy as she slides into her seat for the *Beowulf* postmortem in honors English. Mr. Whiddicomb has our papers graded, so he promised that today he'd discuss them first thing before moving on to discuss the first few chapters of *East of Eden*. While I generally like Steinbeck (I would never admit it to my friends, but I must say I think *Of Mice and Men* is a killer book—pardon the pun), *East of Eden* is just way, way long.

Does Mr. Whiddicomb not realize that we all have five or six other teachers wanting us to do homework every night, and that slogging through such a long book eats up all our other homework time?

Amy shrugs as she pulls out her copy of *East of Eden*—spine uncracked—then takes a Diet Dr Pepper out of her backpack and pops it open. "I ran late this morning. Note I brought along the true Breakfast of Champions."

"Don't you have that every morning?" I say, acting as casual as I can. "Hey, I tried calling you yesterday. Just got the voice mail."

She shifts in her chair and mutters something about how she's sorry she didn't get back to me, but she didn't check her messages until late. I think that's what she said. She seems really distracted.

"You okay?" I ask. Rachel must've said something really and truly horrid about me. "You seem ticked off at—"

"I just don't want to get in trouble," she hisses, then faces forward as Mr. Whiddicomb starts to speak.

I take a long sip of the iced coffee I picked up at Seattle's Best on the way to school, then start paying attention too. After a while, I glance over at Amy. For someone who hated *Beowulf* and hasn't even started *East of Eden*, she sure is riveted.

When the bell rings, I tell her how awesome she did at softball Saturday, like during this one play where she dove for the ball and caught it, then underhanded it to second base to pick off a runner for the third out when the bases were loaded. A smile just starts to crack, but then she waves me off, telling me it was nothing and that she needs to get to her next class early to discuss something with the teacher.

"Amy." I put a hand on her elbow once we're out in the hall and have a few feet of space, so I can talk to her without being heard by anyone else. "If you're mad at me about something, just spit it out. Please."

"It's not that—"

"Yeah, it is." I can see it in her whole body. She's tense when I touch her, and I get the feeling she did about a million bicep curls last night. I don't think this is simply about the Billy thing, not unless Rachel made the situation out to be way worse than it really is. But maybe Rachel really is hurt—and if she is, I need to know.

Or what if it's Sean? Could Sean have e-mailed Amy? Or Rachel or Kendra? It's entirely possible he's been e-mailing or calling them and pleading his case. Not his usual modus operandi, but definitely possible if he's really hurt.

She turns to the side and lets out a big Dr Pepper burp, which draws a couple of cheers from people walking past. "Chloe, you know me." Her voice is low as she continues. "I get mad, I get over it. I don't even know if I'm mad, anyway."

"About what?!"

"Trust me, now is not the time for me to talk about this. I need to think."

I look her square in the eye. If it's possible to convey years of friendship and trust in a look, well, I'm trying my best to do it. Working to sound as calm and focused as possible, I ask, "Could you at least give me a clue?"

She stares at me for a second, then looks down to pick at an imaginary hangnail, which she always does when she's nervous. I'm about to say something to try to get her to spill, but she just shakes her head. "I gotta get to class. Don't worry about it, Chloe. It's probably not as big a deal as I'm making it out to be in my head. We'll talk later, okay? Promise."

Before I can argue, she turns and walks down the hall.

During fifth period the computer lab is totally packed. Probably because it's a Monday and it's far enough into the quarter that everyone seems to have papers due at the same time. I get there before Billy and manage to snag a computer, but it's not at our usual window spot—or even a computer with an empty seat next to me.

"Man, this sucks," he says when he comes in, his backpack slung over one shoulder. "I had a feeling it'd be bad today."

"Yeah, everyone with stuff due and passes in hand. I got here as early as I could, but I couldn't get two seats together."

He stands there for a few secs, right behind me, and for the first time, I'm uncomfortable with him. His glasses are dirty in one corner, and I'm tempted to point it out, but don't. I don't know why—

it's like he's looking past me or something. Beyond the milky white spot on his right lens, toward something that isn't even there. Then he looks at me, and the feeling is gone. He's smiling and his usual self.

"It's no biggie," he tells me. "I figured it'd be crowded today, so I arranged to spend the period with my faculty sponsor." He goes on to explain that they're planning out a project to do with velocity and mass on the moon and a bunch of variables that I don't even want to understand.

Before I can ask how things went at his house after I left on Saturday night, he's gone, handing a note to the lab monitor and then sliding out the door.

I turn back to my computer, feeling unsettled. He didn't seem mad at me or anxious to get out of the room. He even sounded happy about his project, like he wanted to tell me about it just to share the thrill with someone. But there was a bad vibe to the whole thing, one I doubt had anything to do with our kiss, even though he didn't mention it.

I click on the little icon to open my research file, trying to assemble my random notes on the roots of the Arab-Israeli conflict into some sort of order. As I read about the misunderstandings and shared history between various groups, I get the sudden, horrid feeling that I'm gonna be in even deeper than Amy can creatively describe if I don't manage to put all the random conflicts of my life into order.

I hate the smell of the Vista Verde girls' locker room. The worst part is that I don't know *why* it smells so bad. I mean, my bathroom at home always smells like whatever shampoo or soap I've just used, or maybe like hair spray if I've bothered. My towels hang to dry instead of being wadded up in the corner, and they get washed regularly. I clean on a schedule that would appall Martha Stewart, but isn't so sporadic that I worry about anyone seeing it and being icked out.

But the locker room here? Despite regular cleaning (daily), lots of nice-smelling products (a plethora of shampoo and conditioners, not to mention shower gel from a dispenser that you'd actually use), and towels that get one use and then get washed that night, it reeks. It constantly smells like something very wet died in here. My inability to pinpoint the source of the smell deeply disturbs me.

Amy agrees with me, but tolerates it because she's a total jock. On the other hand, Kendra and Rachel try to avoid the place entirely simply because of the smell.

So after school, when I head in to change after an extra-long cross-country practice, I stop cold in the locker room doorway when I see Kendra and Rachel sitting at the end of the bench, deep in discussion. Amy's at the end of the row of lockers, just past where they're sitting, and she looks angry—though at whom, I can't tell. She's wrapped in a towel, but keeps glancing at Kendra and Rachel every few seconds, giving them the death look while she arranges bottles of shampoo and body wash in her shower basket.

"Hey, Chloe," Rachel says in a loud voice when she finally sees me. Instantly, both Amy and Kendra turn to look at me. Their faces both have that sick look of someone who's been breathing locker room air too long.

"Hey," I say, trying to play it cool. I weave past the rest of the softball players, who are either packing their gear or headed for the showers, then gesture to Rachel and Kendra, who stand out in their school clothes. "What's the deal?"

"We need to talk," Rachel says as Amy stalks past her, toward the shower. "Do you have to be anywhere right now?"

"I don't have to be home till seven. Dad's working late. But if you want to go out, I should take a shower first." I force myself to be as calm as possible as I open my locker and make sure I have all the necessary stuff, since I generally shower at home. "Can I ask what it's about?"

Rachel opens her mouth to say something, but at that moment the cheerleaders come through the back door to the locker room and head toward our end of the bench. Even though I know they have to be tired from all the kicking and back handsprings they do on the field, and from practicing pyramid after pyramid, they're all singing aloud—the same obnoxious new cheer they were working on the whole time I was running at cross-country practice—

and totally oblivious to the presence of any-one but themselves. Of course, Margot's the loudest of all. Probably because she writes most of their cheers, a tidbit she tends to drop whenever a guy says something complimentary about any of the routines.

Kendra puts a hand on Rachel's elbow. Rachel glances toward Margot, then says, "Um, how about later?"

I nod, then strip (which I hate doing in front of them, even though I've known them forever) and head to the showers, holding the towel around me so tight, my fingers hurt.

I wish we had shower stalls like some of the other, newer high schools have. We were supposed to get them over the summer, but apparently the budget ran out before they were able to renovate the locker room. Of course.

Can I say it for the record? Communal showers suck.

I hang my towel on a free hook, then go inside and take a lightning-fast shower. Amy, who usually takes her sweet time once she decides she feels like showering at school instead of at home, is unusually quick too. She's out before I even finish shampooing. Whether it's to avoid me or the impending cheerleader shower stampede, I can't tell.

When I get back to my locker, Kendra's talking to a cheerleader friend of hers—I think they go to church together—over in the far corner. Amy's focused on finding clothes in her locker, and Rachel's sitting on the bench right beside mine. She has her chemistry book open on the bench and a notebook in her lap, but her pencil is still and she's staring at me.

I try to think of something normal to say, but I can't. And stupid me, I can't take the silence from her, either, so I whisper so only Rachel can hear, "I've been meaning to talk to you, too. I called you yesterday. A few times."

"My mom told me."

"Oh."

She pushes off the bench as if it's a great effort, then leans against the locker next to mine, flipping her pencil around in her fingers. While I fasten my bra and rummage through my locker looking for my panties, she says, "So? What was it you wanted to talk about?"

I glance past her, toward Amy and Kendra, then focus on her. "I wanted to know what's up with you and Billy."

Her eyebrows shoot up. "With *me* and Billy?"

"Um, yeah." I think my throat's going to cinch shut. "I know you've been scoping him out, but I wasn't sure how serious you were. Or are. I mean, I know things are looking good with Fort Collins Pete, too. And with Gorgeous Jake."

"Was there a particular reason you wanted to ask?" She's not whispering anymore. Behind her, I see Kendra's gaze jerk in our direction.

"Well, you know I was with Sean for a long time, so I'm not good at knowing how to handle these things." There has to be a better way to say this. "But I'm starting to like Billy too, so I wanted to talk to you about everything."

"Really."

Man, she's loud. The cheerleaders are finishing up their showers and are slowly filtering back in, so I say very quietly, "I would never risk our friendship over a guy, so I didn't want to do anything about Billy—or even think about him—until I knew for sure whether you're interested."

I take a deep breath and try to read her expression. But I can't. She looks like she hasn't even heard me, like she's waiting for me to say something else.

"Maybe we should talk about this somewhere else," I say. I roll my eyes in the direction of the cheerleaders and the few softball players who are still left. "Otherwise, we're going to be the focus of gossip central tomorrow, you know?"

"Oh, I'm sure." She twists her pencil around in her fingers, then taps it against the locker next to mine. "So, Chloe, when did you figure this out? Yesterday? Or was it about five minutes after leaving DIA?"

"Hey, guys." Kendra comes up behind Rachel and puts a hand on Rachel's shoulder. "Why don't we go for coffee? Like, *now*?"

"No, I don't think so." Rachel's cheeks go from her usual blusher-enhanced pink to a deep red. "I don't think I can stand to sit next to Miss Perfect here. Little Miss Everybody Wants Me. I don't think I'm pretty enough to hang with her. Might scare the guys off or something."

"Come on," Kendra says. Even though I can tell she's pissed at me too, she's working hard to keep Rachel from exploding.

"Lemme get dressed. I'll hurry, okay?" I look at Rachel, trying to convey how much I really want to make things right. "I just need to find my underwear." I grab my shirt, then my jeans and socks, but I don't see my panties, what with all the extra cross-country clothes piled up in my locker. I need to clean the thing out more often.

"Here they are, you idiot." Rachel sticks her pencil into my locker and fishes out my undies. I reach out to grab them from where they're dangling on her pencil, but she yanks it away, which of course sends them sailing across the room. "You know, I can't get over you," she hisses.

Then there's a collective gasp in the locker room as my panties end their flight by sticking to the locker room wall.

Eight

I stare at the shell-pink silk fabric attached to the wall, petrified. All I can think to myself as the locker room goes silent is, *Breathe, breathe, breathe.*

The sixth-grade "you could model" incident was nothing. Bumpy tile grout plus easy-to-snag fabric equals social disaster.

Rachel and Kendra stare at the wall, their hands over their mouths and their eyes wide. I turn to look over at Amy, who's frozen in place with her brush halfway through her long, wet hair, looking as horrified as I feel.

At least she's dressed. I'm half naked, my panties are essentially Velcroed to the wall, and the entire cheerleading squad is staring at me.

I have to *do* something.

"Well, guess that says it all, doesn't it?" Rachel says, recovering. She leans closer and adds, "The prettiest girls are always the sluttiest ones. Even the ones you think you really know and trust. The minute Sean left, you just figured you'd help yourself to whatever guys you wanted, huh? No matter who got hurt?"

"That's not fair, and it's not true," I protest. The cheerleaders and the last few softball players are starting to whisper back and forth, so I hope they can't hear what I'm saying. Still, I can feel tears filling my eyes and I can't stop them. If I blink, I know they're going to run down my face. Faking a need to towel-dry my hair, I swipe at my eyes.

What has gotten into her? I've never known Rachel to be so nasty, even at her angriest.

But more important than Rachel at the immediate moment: How can I casually go get my undies? And once I do, should I wear them? Trash them and go commando?

I immediately dismiss that idea—

someone would probably fish them out of the garbage and do who-knows-what with them. Send them up the flagpole or hang 'em on the football field's uprights, most likely. But will it be worse to put them on and endure the snickers that will inevitably follow? Or go home in jeans with nothing under them since I don't have a backup pair of underwear in my locker?

"Let's go!" Kendra hisses at me and Rachel. "This is out of control!"

And, I'm acutely aware, we have an audience that includes Margot deVries. I am so so so screwed socially.

I ask Rachel in a voice that practically begs her to give me the benefit of the doubt, "Please, can we go?"

After I explain everything to Rachel, I'm going to ask Dad if I can transfer. I can't ever set foot in this locker room—let alone this high school—again.

"I'm going home. She can go to hell," Rachel hisses, with a dismissive gesture in my direction. She grabs her chemistry book off the bench and loops her Coach purse— a soft lavender one I gave her on her last birthday—over her shoulder, then slams out the back door to the parking lot.

"I'm going to make sure she's okay," Margot announces, then follows her out. How that evil rat bitch got dressed so fast, I don't know. Kendra shoots me a look that says, *This is very, very bad!* and then goes chasing them both, presumably to do damage control.

Amy picks up Rachel's pencil from where it fell on the floor, then walks over to where my panties are slowly starting to fall away from the wall and hooks them with the pencil. She holds them out to me. "Here."

"Thank you," I tell her. But when I look at her and see the doubt on her face, I feel the tears start to burn my eyes all over again.

"Don't thank me," she says, her voice barely audible as I step into my panties despite the smothered giggles coming from the cheerleaders' direction. "I'm still trying to figure you out, Chloe. Does this mean it's true about Billy? How could you do it?"

"I tried calling Rachel all day yesterday," I whisper. "I didn't want to do anything without talking to her first."

Amy stares at me like I've grown a second head. "Just get dressed," she says.

"We'll talk while you drive me home. Rachel was my ride."

I yank on my jeans and shoes, not bothering to take the extra ten seconds with socks. I stuff everything in my backpack, and we walk out the back door as fast as possible. The instant it shuts behind us, I hear a scream of laughter, several howls of "Oh, my God!" and at least one distinct "I always figured she was a ho."

"There's something humorous in this, I'm sure," I tell Amy.

"Yeah, real late-night-comedian material," she says.

It's all I can do not to be physically sick. But I can't let Amy see how devastated I feel, not until I know what she's thinking. I try to focus on the gray-black surface of the asphalt, on getting out my car keys without dropping them, on setting my backpack very carefully in the backseat. Anything but the events of the last ten minutes.

Neither of us say another word until a very Amy-like expletive leaves my mouth while I'm backing out of the parking spot, because that's when I see Rachel leaning against her car, with Margot standing on one side of her. Margot's rubbing Rachel's back and making obviously fake expressions of concern, shaking her head and saying something while Rachel nods.

The fact that Rachel's tolerating it scares me. Apparently it's scaring Kendra, too, since she's standing off to the other side of Rachel, staring at Margot as if Lucifer himself had descended on Vista Verde High's parking lot.

"Well, shit on my cheerleader skirt," Amy grumbles as I drive past them. "Now you've driven her right into the hands of the enemy. Good going."

I don't say anything. I mean, what *can* I say? Billy kissed me, and I'm sorry? Because really, I'm not. I mean, I'm sorry everyone is so pissed, but in my gut, did I really *do* anything wrong?

I should have talked to Rachel first, true. But, for one, I had no idea Billy would kiss me when I went over to play poker, since I didn't think we'd be alone at all, and for two, you'd think Rachel would give me the benefit of the doubt here. Especially since Billy isn't her boyfriend and hasn't ever made the slightest move on her.

Not to mention that she was out with Pete and Gorgeous Jake Saturday night.

My complete humiliation turns to anger as I watch in my rearview mirror while Margot gets all friendly with Rachel. What would possess Rachel to buy her fake compassion?

"Don't scream at me," I say to Amy as I turn my Honda out of the lot. "But I really don't get all of this."

"You don't?"

"Okay, I understand she's pissed about Billy, but . . . well, why is she *so* pissed? And why are you pissed? This is all out of proportion." And since they can't possibly know that Billy and I kissed, I add, "What exactly have I done?"

"You lied to us about Sean, and in the meantime, you're scamming on every guy we're interested in."

Huh? "I haven't lied about Sean, other than to not tell you about the breakup right away." We pull up to a stop sign, and I take the chance to look over at her. "And whaddya mean, every guy 'we're' interested in?"

"Um . . ." Her expression suddenly goes to panic.

"You never did tell me who it is you're crushing on," I say, "and I asked you straight out if it's Billy. So what the——"

"It's not Billy."

It's not? Whoa. *"Sean?"*

"God, no." She lets out a huff of air. "No offense, but, uh, *no.* Norcross isn't my type. And he's a zillion miles away."

True, she did say she sees whoever it is regularly. "Then who? Who could I possibly be scamming on? Because whoever it is you think I'm after, if it's not Billy or Sean, well, I can promise you that I'm not. And I'm not even 'scamming'"—I make quote marks in the air over the steering wheel—"on either of them. It's totally over with Sean, and I don't know if anything is going to happen with Billy and me at this point. Even if I knew how to *scam* on him." I may be fairly clueless about guys, but I can't imagine Billy wanting to be with me after he hears about the locker room incident.

She leans back in the seat as far as she can, with her elbow on the armrest and her hand laced through her dark, wet hair. I notice she missed a spot of red dirt on her elbow, so I make a joke about it in a half-hearted attempt to ease the tension.

She actually smiles, wrenches her elbow so she can get a better look, then swipes it away.

"Look," she says after a deep breath. "I know you've been ga-ga-stupid in love with Sean for years. So before I tell you about me, why don't you tell me why you don't want to get back together with Sean?"

"I already told you guys."

"I wanna hear it again."

So I explain, in painful detail, how he broke my heart when he dumped me. How I questioned everything I've done the last two years. How good it felt once I started running—which she pushed me to do—because it made me realize that I didn't have to be part of some Chloe-Sean entity to feel good about myself. That I'd actually closed off a big chunk of myself just to spend more time with Sean, and I'd missed the chance to get to spend time with other people.

"Like Billy?"

"Yeah. And you guys. That's the biggie.

How many weekends have you gone shopping or to movies without me because I was busy with Sean? I don't want to miss out on that anymore. So when Sean called yesterday morning—"

"Sean called you?"

"Yeah. I asked him to. I thought we needed to talk after the e-mails."

She starts chewing on her hangnail again, and I reach across the car to push her finger away from her mouth. A very mom-like move, but whatever.

"What?"

Amy slides a glance at me. "Rachel said that you refused to talk to Sean. That you were nasty to him."

"Whoa. So not true."

We're almost to Amy's house, so I ask her if I can detour into the Burger King parking lot. Once I pull into an empty spot, I cut the engine and give Amy the play-by-play of my conversation with Sean, including the confusing parts where he seemed to think I was running cross-country to meet more guys—and emphasized that I didn't say the slightest thing to him that could be construed as nasty. Even when I started to suspect that the only reason he wanted to get back together was because he thought I might be seeing someone.

"And," I finish, "I showed you guys all the e-mails between us before the phone call, so I don't know why Rachel would say that. Unless not getting back together with him is her definition of 'being nasty,' which sounds pretty extreme to me."

"You're right. It does sound kind of extreme. Wow." I can tell from her face that she believes me—that either Rachel's been feeding her a line of bull, or someone's been feeding it to Rachel, who wanted to believe it.

Frankly, I'm wondering that too. Where would Rachel have gotten that idea?

Amy picks a loose strand of hair from her shirt, then lowers the window and flicks it out. As she rolls the window back up, she says, "So you're telling me it's totally over with Sean—"

"Totally."

"And the only guy you have any interest in right now is Billy?"

"Yes. But I think that's not happening."

She goes back to picking hair off her shirt, but this time, it's imaginary. "And there's no one else?" she asks.

"What, I'm not getting myself into enough trouble already?"

"Good point." She drops her hands into her lap and looks sideways at me. "Then I have to ask. Why were you hugging Eric Biedermeyer? Is there something there?"

"Eric? No way in . . ." And then it dawns on me.

"Yeah, you know what I'm talking about. After the cross-country meet on Saturday, you two were looking awfully friendly. He even picked you up and was swinging you around, and you two were laughing—"

"I remember. He was on an adrenaline rush and excited about how I ran. But not excited about *me*. There's a big difference." Though in retrospect, seeing it from the outside, I understand why someone might think it looked like we were more than just friends.

Apparently, I have to be careful about appearances.

"So that's who you've been crushing on,

huh?" I turn in the seat so I'm facing her. "I thought you couldn't stand him."

She blushes, and I can't help but smile. "You don't change, do you, Amy? You can talk to any guy except the one you're interested in."

"Especially if he's interested in my best friend. And my best friend is utterly cool and beautiful beyond words."

"Trust me, he's not interested in me. Geez! And *this* is why you hopped on the Rachel bandwagon and wanted me to get back with Sean so bad?"

"Well . . ." She shrugs. "I should've just told you. But Rachel seemed so certain you were doing this Sean-rebound thing and were after whomever you could get." She gives me the most apologetic look I've ever seen from her. "I blew it, big-time."

"I should pop you one in the forehead."

She laughs. "Yeah, well, you know I could pop you back harder."

I start mentally replaying my conversations with Eric, then say, "You know, you were thinking he might be interested in someone? Now that I think about it, he might be interested in *you*. He's always asking about you. Like if you're mad at him. And when we're running at practice, when we get to the part of the trail behind the softball field, he's always scoping you out."

"Yeah, right."

"Really. Wow. You know, how could I not have seen it? Amy, he's got to be interested. Remember when I told you that he said if we wanted to hang out with him after practice sometime, that'd be cool, even though I'm not with Sean anymore? When he said that, he specifically mentioned you." I lean over and grab her arm, I'm so pumped about this now. "He said, 'I meant what I said about you and Amy. . . .' I can't believe I didn't pick up on that!"

"No way. No way!" A smile pulls at the corners of her mouth, but she tries to hide it with her hand.

"Yes way. In fact, after that hug he gave me, he saw you walking into the locker room. I was watching you 'cause you looked angry. Now I know why. But he was watching too, 'cause he asked, 'Is that Amy?' I just shrugged him off, because if you were angry about something, I didn't think it was his business. Geez, I'm such an idiot!"

"Why?"

"Because I should have known! You two would be perfect together. He's a really nice guy. Plus, both of you are athletic and smart, and he's actually tall enough for you."

She laughs at that one, and for the first time since I got up this morning, I feel genuinely happy. Like something good might come out of all this mess.

"Let me talk to Eric at practice tomorrow—"

"You can't tell him!"

"I won't." I lean back against the door and pull my knees up so I'm more comfortable. "I'll just feel him out. I'll be smooth about it, I promise."

"Okay." Her smile is about a hundred watts. "Thank you."

Well, at least one of us has hope for a romantic future.

We're quiet for a moment, knowing what comes next. Finally, Amy says, "So what are you going to do about Rachel?"

I shrug. "Try to talk to her, I guess. If she'll take my calls. I could always show up at her house, I s'pose." I jerk my thumb toward the drive-thru. "I'm starving. Mind if we get something?"

She waves for me to go ahead, handing me a ten and telling me what to order for her. Once we're settled again—and the car is filled with French fry odor—I ask her why Rachel is so angry about Billy. "It's not like they're going out or anything," I add. "Not that I'd ever go after a guy she's interested in, but you know, even if I did, this is just . . ." I picture my underwear stuck to the tile and I shudder. I soooo need to get home and change. This pair is going in the trash. Maybe even into the fireplace. "This is *bad*."

"She'll get over it," Amy says. "And for what it's worth, I'm really sorry."

"It's not your fault that the grout in the locker room is heavily texturized," I say between bites of cheeseburger. You'd think the image would kill my appetite, but no. I think I need to drown my depression over what's bound to happen with Billy—as in *nothing*—in mood-altering amounts of sodium and partially hydrogenated oils.

"No, but I was mad at you too. When Rachel took me out shopping Sunday and went on and on about how you were after every guy on the planet, and I'd just seen you hugging Eric the day before, *and* I kept seeing you guys running together and him talking to you nonstop . . . anyway, I should have known the day I asked you about it after the first cross-country practice that you were telling the truth. And I should have known better with Rachel. She's had this jealousy thing going on with you for years."

I swallow hard, and a piece of cheeseburger goes down the wrong way. I croak out, *"Years?"*

She picks up my soda and orders me to drink. Once my throat's clear, I say, "I haven't even known Billy for years!"

"This isn't about Billy. And it's not about that Jake guy chasing you out of the party and driving off with you—which she did notice, by the way."

I was afraid of that. "He came out of the party and pounded on my window. I thought he wanted to ask me about her, so I gave him a ride home. Jerk asked me out instead. I told him I was taken. Trying not to be rude about turning him down, you know? And then—get this—after I dropped him off, he never went into his house. He got in his truck and went right back to the party. I was in a drive-thru near his house and saw him go by."

Amy rolls her eyes and makes a snarfing sound. "Rachel told me he came back. He claimed he went to get his truck in case Pete got too plowed to drive."

"Um, in that case, couldn't he have taken Pete's keys and offered to drive everyone home in Pete's car? Not that Pete was even drinking—"

"Exactly what Rachel said. Jake's story didn't wash."

What an idiot. Jake might be gorgeous, but he couldn't lie worth a damn.

"Anyway, I guess Billy went up to his room early, saying he was tired, and the rest of 'em just watched football the rest of the night."

I cringe. So not Rachel's scene.

"By the next morning, her bitch switch had definitely flipped," Amy says between sips of her Diet Coke. "I've never seen her so mad. What you got in the locker room—well, at first—was really calm. She was ballistic when I went shopping with her yesterday."

I finish a fry, then stuff the rest of them back in the bag. I can't stomach them anymore.

Amy reaches over and takes the rest of my fries without bothering to ask. "Rachel's probably never told you, and I know I haven't, but she had a huge thing for Sean back in eighth grade. That's what I meant when I said she's had this thing with you going on for years."

I stare at Amy. The rush of Burger King sodium's affecting my brain.

"No, really," she says. "It's true."

"I had no clue. None." Back then, Rachel never talked about guys. What she did talk about was everything else. School. TV. Sports. Gossip. You name it. Her mouth never stopped.

Once, at a sleepover, we asked Alyssa to stand behind her with a stopwatch and time her longest pause in conversation. Alyssa, being Alyssa, refused. But Amy eventually did it, and Rachel topped out at fifteen seconds without opening her mouth. And that was after nearly an hour of being timed. But never once in those years did she mention any particular guy.

"I didn't know either," Amy says. "She mentioned it once last year, in an offhanded way. But I got the feeling that it was really hard on her when you hooked up with Sean. It was like it changed her entire reality."

I frown, since my mouth's full of cheeseburger, and Amy continues. "We were semi-outcasts back then, remember? You were incredibly pretty, which made you acceptable, but you had that whole 'I could model' thing following you around, making people think you were a snot. I was a jock, which has its good side and its bad side. Especially since I *looked* like a jock. I had total boy hair back then."

"Isn't that style 'in' now, though?" I can't help but tease her. "You'd look good with helmet hair again!"

"Thanks," she says with an eyeroll. "We weren't the only ones, though. Kendra was so quiet back then that we were the only ones who really knew her—how smart and nice she is. And Rachel might've had style, even back then, but she also had the motor-mouth thing. And she and Margot had been really good friends right before that, until Margot got all hot and heavy about that one guy and started ignoring her. Do you remember that guy? Summer between seventh and eighth grade. Whuzzisname?"

I totally spaced the Rachel-Margot connection. It feels like ancient history. I rack my brain, and finally say, "Wasn't it Deacon? Or Dylan? Something like that?"

"Declan! Remember Rachel and Margot had some big fight after Margot hooked up with him—as much as you can hook up in seventh grade, anyway—and by the time Declan and Margot broke up, Rachel was hanging with us, and she didn't want to hear Margot's apology."

"You sure that's why Margot and Rachel stopped hanging out? I thought the fight was 'cause Margot decided over the summer to go out for cheerleading and Rachel didn't want to. Right about then was when Margot started getting all popular, remember?"

Amy raises an eyebrow, considering. "I guess that's possible. None of us asked Rachel about it then, I don't think. But, wait . . . she told me last year—when she told me about her crush on Sean—that she didn't say anything about it to us before 'because of the Margot episode.' Those were her exact words. I bet anything she liked that guy and Margot went after him. Doesn't that make sense?"

"That does sound like something Margot would do. I didn't think she was that bad back then, though."

"I wasn't really paying attention," Amy admits.

"Do you think Kendra knows the whole story?"

Amy shrugs. "We can call her later and ask. Don't want to call now, though—she's probably still with Rachel. And Miss Hellspawn."

I sit back for a minute, waiting for Amy to finish eating. No matter what else happens, I'm glad the two of us are cool again. And I tell her so.

Her cheeks go pink. "That's why I didn't want to say anything in class today. I didn't want to go all girly—cat fight on you unless I was certain you deserved it."

"Appreciated."

As I back out of the space and head toward Amy's house, a thought occurs to me. "If Rachel had such a crush on Sean, I wonder why she didn't go nutso about it when Sean and I hooked up?"

Amy's brow furrows. When we get to a stoplight, I turn and look at her. "I think," she says slowly, "it could be because you didn't rub the boyfriend thing in her face the way Margot probably did. You treated Rachel the same as always. And really, if she dissed you back then, right after her blowout with Margot, who else would she hang with?"

"You know, I bet it was pretty awful for her." I think back, trying to put myself in Rachel's shoes. "It never occurred to me that she'd worry about our friendship changing if I got a boyfriend—let alone a boy she'd been interested in."

I hit the gas when the light turns green, then turn into Rachel's neighborhood, past the big sign warning drivers about SLOW CHILDREN. That sign always pisses off Amy—she even climbed the post with a screwdriver and managed to take it down once when we were in fourth or fifth grade, hoping they'd replace it with one that said CHILDREN AT PLAY or with a speed limit. But they only replaced it with a bigger

SLOW CHILDREN sign. With impenetrable screws to hold it in place.

"I'd have kicked your ass if you'd acted that way, even if I am a Slow Child," she says, her gaze following mine to the bright yellow sign. "When you started going out with Sean, it didn't occur to me that you would. I guess because the two of us"—she waves a fry between us—"have always been so tight. Anyway, by the time Rachel mentioned all this to me last year, she'd been over Sean for a long time. But . . . and this just now occurred to me . . . maybe she never got over Margot deVries?"

As soon as the words leave Amy's mouth, I know it's the truth. The reason Rachel asked Alyssa about 'who do you hate the most?' at the assembly and went on and on about how everyone hates pretty girls. The reason that less than an hour ago she told me that all pretty girls were slutty, even the ones you think you can trust.

It all went back to Margot.

Rachel feeling like Margot rejected her. Rachel worrying that I might reject her too.

"No wonder she went out of control

back there in the locker room." I picture Rachel's face, trying to remember her exact expression when she was talking to me. There had been sadness there as much as anger—but I had been so focused on trying to find my undies and get out of there, at least before they hit the wall, that I hadn't picked up on the obvious. "She thinks it's happening all over again."

"So go convince her it's not."

I pull into Amy's driveway and let the car idle. "It won't be easy. I mean, I can't exactly ring her doorbell and say, 'Hey, I think this is all a childhood problem. . . .' Not without her slamming the door in my face."

"But it's worth a try. And if it doesn't work, try again. She'll figure out that you're sincere. And if she doesn't . . ." Amy shrugs. "Then know you've done your best and that this is something Rachel needs to work out for herself."

Right. Like that ever works with anyone.

Amy unsnaps her seat belt and leans over to give me a hug, which she hardly ever does. She's just not the huggy type.

She tells me to call her and let her know how it goes with Rachel, then climbs out. She shuts the door, and I'm just about to back out when she grabs the handle and opens it. Leaning in, she says, "Hey, and don't give up on WooWoo just yet either."

I can't help but snort. "Oh, yeah, he'll want to go out with Underwear on the Wall Girl. Sure." I mimic the snotty little voice I heard coming from the locker room when we left: "'I always figured she was a ho!'"

"I won't give up on Eric. You don't give up on Billy. We're both gonna be Charlie Sheen here. Deal?"

I smile back. This is why she's my best friend. "Deal."

Nine

I must be certifiable.

One, I have wet hair and zero makeup.

Two, I'm sockless.

Three, I'm wearing The Underwear.

Four, I have French fry breath, compounded by post-cross-country breath.

Five, I already rang the bell, so it's too late to run. The front door of Rachel's house has a big glass window in it, so I'd be spotted making my getaway.

"Chloe! How are you, sweetheart?" A waft of vanilla hits my nose as Mrs. Nielsen opens the front door of their immaculate house. I wonder if she's been making cookies (she's totally a cookie-making mom) or if it's her perfume. Either way, it's so fresh and pure and so unlike my house that I feel even grubbier in comparison.

"Fine, Mrs. Nielsen." *Lie, lie, lie.* "I'm not interrupting dinner, am I?" It comes out sounding like I'm here to report for a prison sentence instead of swinging by to see one of my best friends. Mrs. Nielsen doesn't seem to notice, though.

"Of course not." She waves me in. "Rachel's father won't be home for another hour, so it won't be on the table till then."

"Oh. Okay." So much for a reprieve.

"She's in her room. Why don't you go on up?"

She's so smiley and kind, I want to hug her. Like a last good-bye before I see the executioner. Instead, I tell her thanks and take the stairs in twos. If I linger in the front hall any longer, I'll either find another excuse and chicken out or Rachel will hear me talking and she'll throw me out.

I'd rather Mrs. Nielsen not witness anything violent.

I get to the top of the stairs, take a deep breath, then knock just under the pink wooden RACHEL sign hanging on her door.

There's a scuffling sound, like she's cleaning up or something, then a "Yeah . . . come on in!"

I can tell from the casual tone that she thinks it's her brother or her mom. I'm not sure if that's good or bad.

Who am I kidding? Either way she's gonna hit the roof the instant she sees me.

I open the door and meet her gaze, but don't step in. "Um, hey. It's me."

She's sitting on her bed, and it looks like she just finished doing her nails. She's barefoot, and her toes are the same electric red shade as her fingertips. I half expect her to throw something at me, wet nails or not. But she just shrugs. "So come inside already."

Okay. So far, so good. Maybe she's calmed down.

I shut the door behind me so if things get bad, Mrs. Nielsen doesn't hear. I wait for Rachel to say something first, but when it's clear she's not going to, I tell her, "That was a nasty scene in the locker room."

"You think?" She looks down and picks at her big toe, removing a flicker of polish off the cuticle.

I take a deep breath. *In, out. In, out.* Shoot . . . that only makes me taste my own French fry breath. "I know you're probably waiting for me to say I'm sorry, Rachel, but I think this goes both ways. Yes, I should have made more of an effort to talk to you about the whole Billy thing. To tell you I'd been invited to his house. I know that. But Jake wasn't my fault, and you shouldn't have jumped to conclusions. He asked me for a ride, and I thought it was so he could get info about you."

"Um-hmmmm." She reaches behind a row of various nail polish colors on her nightstand, grabs an orange stick, then runs it along the edge of her other big toe.

You'd think I was reading my history of the Middle East paper aloud to her or something, for all she seems to care.

Well, if she's gonna be this way, I'm just gonna blurt it out. "I think you know you don't have a right to be mad at me for *liking* Billy, though. And I think you're angry about Sean because, for whatever reason, you think I've been mean to him. But I think the biggest issue—bigger than any guy issues you might or might not have with me—is Margot deVries."

She freezes mid-cuticle but doesn't look up. "You *were* mean to Sean. Like, horrid. He loved you, and he might've been a jerk right when he left, but he apologized."

She glances up at me, and the look on her face is cold. Hard. "You never appreciated him. It doesn't matter how many years you get picked as 'Best Looking' for class favorites in the yearbook, or how often people say you have the prettiest green eyes and dark hair. You could be the real Cleopatra, for all I care, instead of a carbon copy. You were lucky to have him."

"You're right." I lean back against the door frame as she goes back to working on her pedicure. This whole conversation is making my stomach pitch—well, the French fry grease doesn't help—but at least now we're getting somewhere. "I was lucky to have him. But I did appreciate him. I appreciated him just as much as you would have if he'd hooked up with you instead of me."

She looks up at me, tossing the orange stick in the general direction of her trash can. It bounces off the rim and falls into a pair of tennis shoes on the floor. "So the talons come out, huh Chloe? Obviously you've been talking to Amy. Now you're going to rub Sean in my face? Well, let me tell you, I got over that a long, long time ago."

I shake my head. "That's not it at all. I'm just saying I understand why you'd be mad at me about Billy. I didn't know you liked Sean way back then. The fact that you did and then he went out with me . . . and now you're interested in Billy . . . well, it's understandable you wouldn't want Billy with me, given all that history. Especially after that blowup with Margot back in junior high, because I'm guessing now it was about—"

"What happened with me and Margot is none of your beeswax," she says, shooting off the bed and pointing at me. "It's ancient history and you know nothing about it. It doesn't have anything to do with Sean. Or anything to do with why I'm mad at you now."

Ooo-kay. In the most polite, friendly voice I can muster, I say, "Then maybe you can tell me why you really are mad at me?"

At that moment, my brain engages. I

take a subtle glance back at the tennis shoes to see if I saw what I think I saw.

Sure enough, they're too small to be Rachel's. They're also pristine and white and each one has a green stripe on the side. Our school colors.

Cheerleader shoes.

No wonder Rachel doesn't want to get into a discussion about the argument that ended her friendship with Margot.

I don't even register what Rachel's saying—just her angry tone—as my gaze slides toward the bathroom door. It's shut. Ditto on the closet. Margot could be hiding in either place. Probably the scuffling noise I heard when I came in. Since Rachel's bedroom overlooks the front of the house, it's totally possible she saw me pull into the driveway.

I can only imagine the expletives Amy would spew at this point.

". . . and I don't think you've ever appreciated our friendship," Rachel finishes, her hands on her hips. "So don't go trying to blame Margot. This is all about you."

I'm way out of my league here.

"Maybe I should leave, then." My voice

is perfectly level, which amazes me. "But think about what I said. No matter what you believe, I did appreciate Sean, and I want him to be happy. I didn't get back with him because we aren't right for each other anymore. It had nothing to do with Billy, one way or the other."

She's still glaring at me, hands on hips. I can tell she's about to tell me to get the hell out—she just has that look on her face—but I need to finish.

If I don't do it now, she might never give me the chance.

"When you take the time to think about everything I've done, and everything that's happened in our friendship over the last few years, you'll realize I want you to be happy too, Rachel. You're important to me, and you always will be. Even if you did toss my underwear across the locker room."

I think I hear a snort coming from the bathroom, but I can't be sure because Rachel's suddenly coughing.

When she stops, I put a hand on the doorknob, but keep my eyes on hers and say, "I will always be honest with you, Rachel. I know Amy and Kendra feel the same way.

But whether you hang with me in the future, whether you believe a word I'm saying, I want you to find friends you *can* trust. So you know in your heart when they say things like 'Chloe's being nasty to Sean' that it's the truth. That you'll never have to question how they can possibly know that, or why they'd say something like that to you."

And that's when it hits me.

Margot IMed me about my breakup on the first day of school. Not only had her IM been a backhanded 'R U OK?', she'd been almost happy, with her 'heard Sean dumped U at DIA!' And she'd heard before anyone, even Eric Biedermeyer, one of Sean's closest friends. Eric had said Margot had told him about it at lunch.

Because she'd probably heard it straight from Sean.

Sean, who—like all guys—is clueless about Margot, probably didn't think it was any big deal to tell her, especially if she e-mailed him in Connecticut, fishing for info and faking concern.

She's been using that info for her own personal amusement. For *weeks*. Seeing what a mess she can make of Rachel's life—and my life—just because she can.

"Or"—the thought just occurs to me—"when they tell Sean I'm only going out for cross-country to hook up with guys. Think about why they might say something as off the wall as that. What would be the point?"

Rachel's face goes totally, completely white. Before she can say anything, I turn and go. I'll let her work things out with Margot, assuming she's figured out that Margot's been doing this to push her buttons and break up our friendship.

I pull the door shut behind me. I'm tempted to stand there in the hall, listening, but I figure I'd better prove what I said about honesty.

I can't believe what just happened. As I grip the rail, I realize my hands are shaking, and by the time I get to the bottom of the stairs, my heart's pounding about a million miles an hour. I actually jump when Mrs. Nielsen sticks her head out of the kitchen. "That was quick, Chloe."

"Oh. Yeah. I have to get home before dinnertime." Like Dad's actually making something.

She gives me a toothpaste-commercial

smile. "I'm glad you came over." She glances toward the staircase and, in a whisper, she adds, "Margot hasn't been over in years. I was beginning to wonder about the two of them up there!"

"I know what you mean." I can't help but smile back at Mrs. Nielsen. I might not remember much about my own mom, but I'd like to think she was something like Rachel's. Caring and sweet, but not totally naive, either. "I'll see you soon, Mrs. N."

I believe in Rachel enough to think that I will.

"Hey, you're running later than usual. I made chicken." Dad's got the kitchen in full-blown cooking mode—which means he opened a package of preprepared chicken and put it in the oven. He even opened the bagged salad I (optimistically) grabbed at the grocery store last week. The one I was expecting to rot in the fridge, just like nearly every other bagged salad I buy.

"Wow." It's not Mrs. Nielsen's cooking, but to me, it's home. "You even got out real plates instead of paper."

"I need to run the dishwasher tonight, so

what's two more plates? Plus, I felt like eating something other than junk," Dad explains as he pulls the chicken out of the oven with a tattered mitt. "Grab the ketchup and bring it in the family room, please? Our show's on in less than two minutes."

How'd I forget? Monday night.

Well, I know how I forgot. But he'll be really disappointed if I confess that I just had drive-thru with Amy.

We settle on the couch with chicken, salad, and a couple cans of Diet Coke and go through the usual what-do-I-have-for-homework discussion during the commercials.

And wouldn't you know it, at the end of the show, Charlie Sheen gets kicked in the teeth by a girl. Again. This time, the girl sees him horsing around with a bunch of his friends, decides he's a total doofus, and ditches him.

"This is so unrealistic," I tell Dad during the last set of commercials. "No one who gets dumped that many times would want to go out with anyone ever again. But he finds a new girl every week, and he's so optimistic about it!"

Dad grabs my plate and takes it to the dishwasher. Drive-thru or not, I still managed to eat all the chicken. "I don't think it's unrealistic at all," he says. "True, it's a sitcom, so it's a little over the top, but think about it. Are any of the women he's meeting someone you think he should be seeing long-term?"

Hmmmm. "No. Not really."

"Well, there you go. He believes in himself, and he knows what he wants. The story line has them all dumping him, but in real life, don't you think he'd eventually end all those relationships?" He clicks a couple buttons on the dishwasher, then comes back into the family room, where I'm flopped on the couch. "Some of them don't respect his career, some want him for his looks and don't really know him. Some don't like his friends. Some simply aren't right. I think that's pretty much real life."

I cross my arms around my waist. "Are you trying to parent me? Teach me a life lesson?"

"You betcha. Someone has to." He grins, then sits beside me and slings an arm around my shoulder the same way he did after the cross-country meet. "Be patient. Sean wasn't the one, even if he was a great guy. Eventually, you'll find someone who appreciates you for you. Who comes into your life at the right time, unlike Sean. Someone who respects and adores you, and who likes your friends and shares your dreams." He gives my shoulder a squeeze, then rubs his fist against my scalp, making tangles of my hair.

"Dad, cut it out!" He's such a guy sometimes.

He stands up and clicks off the television. "In the meantime, Chloe, enjoy your life the way it is. You're doing well in school, you have some great friends, like Amy, and cross-country's going well." He pauses and shoots me a grin that lets me know he's about to say something dorky. "And, of course, you have me, the best chicken-cookin' Dad in the world."

Yep, dorky. "Unfortunately, I have all your dead ducks in the freezer too."

"And those, too." Since he has to get up early for some kind of financial meeting at work, he heads up to read and get a good night's sleep. I pick up his empty Diet

Coke can and toss it in the recycling bin, then put the ketchup back in the fridge in its usual spot on the door. The house is quiet, other than the soft sounds of Dad moving around upstairs and the *swoosh* of the dishwasher.

My mind instantly goes to the locker room. To my conversation with Amy. To the scene at Rachel's.

Too much drama.

I run my hand over the counter, swiping the crumbs into the sink, and figure that Dad's right: I need to enjoy my life the way it is—focus on things that make me happy. Cross-country. Amy. Dad (assuming I don't look in the freezer). Even Steinbeck, now that I'm into the story.

And, hopefully, Billy will be one of those things in life that make me happy too. But if not, then I'm gonna have to learn to be okay with that.

I think I can do it.

"Un-freaking-believable," Amy whispers as she stands next to my locker, shaking her head over my Rachel update. It feels like the first day of school all over again. I can't focus on what's around me or on what I have coming up in my classes today, because all I can think about is Billy, and how he's going to react when he hears gossip about The Underwear Incident. And he's going to hear. People are staring at me as I wrestle with my locker combo, since it's decided not to work. So I know they'll be talking about me in class, just like they did after Sean dumped me.

It's like déjà vu all over again.

"So did Rachel call you back?" Amy asks. "I mean, did she figure all this out?"

"No, I didn't hear a word." I look sideways at Amy. "And I don't know anything for certain . . . all that stuff with Margot was just a guess on my part."

"I think it's a pretty good guess," comes a voice from behind me. I turn around to see Kendra, looking deadly serious. "You should have seen how, well, *triumphant* Margot looked when she hopped into Rachel's car to ride home with her after you and Amy left. As soon as they got out of the parking lot, I began to wonder."

"So what do you think?" Amy asks.

"Hard to know for sure. But I came to the

same conclusion it sounds like you guys did."

I give up on the locker and face Kendra. "Did you talk to Rachel last night? After you saw her in the parking lot, I mean?"

Kendra's lips form a tight line, and she shakes her head.

"Well," I say, ignoring the fact that most people are now giggling when they go by my locker. "You guys should go to class. Let's forget about Margot and see what happens. Give Rachel time to figure things out for herself."

"I'm not walking to class without you," Amy says.

"Look, you guys, given what happened yesterday—"

"Forget it," Kendra says, reaching past me. "What's your combo? Let me take a crack at it."

I give her the numbers, and she starts spinning. I look from her to Amy. "Thank you, guys. You have no idea what this means to me."

"We're always going to be your friends," Kendra says over her shoulder.

Amy nods and adds, "And Rachel's, too. She'll figure that out soon. I hope."

Kendra pops open my locker, then stands back so I can grab my books for first period honors English. Not that I can concentrate on Steinbeck right now.

"And," Kendra adds, "in the meantime, we'll do our best at damage control. Make it sound like yesterday's locker room thing was all a big joke."

I tell her thanks, even though I know it's one of those things that's beyond damage control. I'm just happy to know that she and Amy are on my side.

We walk down the hall together, and I try not to look as humiliated as I feel when people stare and whisper. I keep my eyes open for Billy, but no luck.

"Things'll work out with Billy," Amy says after Kendra scoots into her trig class, apparently reading my mind. "Be positive. Be Charlie Sheen. If you don't, I'm gonna pop you one on the forehead again."

I smile at her before we walk into Mr. Whiddicomb's room. But not before I duck. Just in case.

I stand outside the door to the computer lab, trying to look as nonchalant as possible, like I belong in the hallway. I can't bring myself to look inside.

Rachel skipped school this morning, but I heard from Amy that someone saw Rachel standing in the office at the end of lunch, giving the receptionist a note. So she's in the building somewhere. And Margot's been talking to everyone in the meantime, repeating the whole locker room story (and probably embellishing it), and, when she gets that whole story out, telling whoever's still listening that I am a horrid person who backstabbed poor, innocent Rachel.

Yeah, right.

Since I know who my friends are, and I know I've survived being a social pariah before, I really only have one concern left.

Billy.

The warning bell rings, and I know I can't put it off any longer. I'm going to have to go inside.

A hand on my arm stops me. "Hey, Chloe."

I turn to see Billy. He looks the same as yesterday, only without the spot on his glasses. "Hey, back."

"Heard you had a rough afternoon yesterday."

"Probably a fair assessment." More like the understatement of the year. I wonder what, exactly, he's heard. And how he's going to handle it.

"Wanna ditch?"

"Come again?" I swear, it's all I can do not to look like I just heard the world is ending. "You? *You* want to ditch?"

And what is he planning to do if I agree?

A smile tugs at one side of his heavenly mouth, and it hits me that I probably won't get to kiss him again.

Once was definitely not enough.

"I'll ask for a library pass, then just not go to the library. You do the same thing." He gestures toward the open door. "She trusts us now, and no one's going to check to make sure we actually go to the library. We'll be back for sixth period."

I don't have anything urgent to do for independent study, so I just shrug and follow his lead. A few minutes later, we're back in the hall, library passes in hand. He starts toward the library and I follow, wondering what he has in mind but too nervous to ask. As we pass the restrooms in senior hall, instead of turning toward the library, he pushes open the exit door, which is the one closest to the parking lot.

"My car's in the second row, but we'll be seen." I point up to the row of classroom windows above us.

"Nope. Come on." He rounds the corner, heading away from the parking lot. For the first time, I notice that he's wearing what Amy and Rachel call Ass Grab Pants. I'm not sure which one of them coined the term—"Ass Grab" sounds more like Amy, but Rachel's the fashionista who names things like pants—but Ass Grab Pants are the kind that, when worn by the right guy, really make you want to, well, grab his ass. They hang just right and fit in all the right places.

And today, Billy's jeans are definitely of the Ass Grab variety. I never could have imagined anyone with Billy's geek tendencies looking so smokin' hot, but the proof is right in front of me.

Of course, when any of us mention to each other that we think a girl is wearing Ass Grab Pants (okay, I can't bring myself to say it out loud since I'm the queen of hangups when it comes to using foul language, but Kendra, Amy, and Rachel have no problem with it), it's because we've noticed all the other girls are calling her a ho and saying she's intentionally trying to get guys' attention when really, all she's doing is wearing pants that make her rear end not look huge.

In other words, it's just us getting ticked off at the old double standard.

I'm so distracted by Billy's Ass Grab Pants that I nearly run into him when he stops and turns around.

"Here." He links his fingers together to form a step, apparently oblivious to the fact that I've been scoping him out. "I'll give you a boost up the ladder. We can sit on the roof."

I glance up, noticing for the first time that a long metal ladder is attached to the side of the building. The bottom rung is about three feet above Billy's head. "Um, if you give me a boost, how are you gonna get up?"

"I'll jump."

"Get outta here."

The confident grin on his face melts my insides. "Go."

I hook my backpack so it's firmly over both shoulders, step into his intertwined fingers, then put my hands on his shoulders. Before I can ask him if he's certain, he's hefting me up into the air. I grab for the bottom rung, then pull up as he pushes my feet from below. A second later, I can hear him coming up the ladder behind me.

He's way stronger than I ever would have guessed.

"We're going to get in so much trouble," I say once we both collapse on the gravel-covered roof. "They'll cancel our independent study if they catch us."

"They won't." He gestures toward the edge, and I'm surprised to see Twinkie wrappers, a smashed beer bottle, a few rain-soaked pieces of notebook paper, and even a few cigarette butts strewn in the gravel. "I see the football players up here every so often, and they've never been caught," he explains. "Most of those guys are not what I'd call subtle about skipping class."

I admit he has a point. Sean used to hang out with a lot of them, so I know that there are a few who aren't exactly bright about this kind of thing. I slowly take a look around. The view is unreal. I can see all the cars in the parking lot and the sports fields beyond that, with the cross-country trail cutting into the evergreens behind them. The course looks a lot shorter from up here.

"C'mon. We should sit. Otherwise, we'll be seen if someone comes into the parking lot and looks up."

We find a clear space next to some air-conditioning units and we drop our backpacks, using them as backrests so we can sit leaning against the gray metal. The sun is bright, but it's not so hot that we cook up here on the roof. Billy yanks a Rockies cap out of his backpack and pulls it on. For a long time we sit in silence, listening to the cars coming and going on the street nearby.

After a few minutes I stop wanting to ask Billy what he heard about me. It's so peaceful, it seems like it'd ruin the mood. I also suspect he wouldn't have brought me up here in the first place if he thought I was a horror of a human being.

"Funny how we can be right on top of the school, yet it seems so far away," Billy says. "Like this morning's classes really happened days ago instead of a couple hours ago."

I scooch up a little against the air conditioner so my eyes are shaded, then turn and smile at him. "I was just thinking the same thing."

He reaches into the side pocket of his backpack and pulls out a pack of cinnamon gum. Without even asking, he holds it out to me. Just like any other day in the computer lab. I smile and grab a piece, then he takes one too. I ball up the wrapper and I'm about to put it in my front jeans pocket when he holds out his palm. "Here. I'll trash it when we go back inside."

I drop it in his open hand. "So I take it you haven't contributed to the Twinkie wrapper graveyard?"

"Nah. Never been up here before. Plus, I'm seriously anti-litter. One of my pet peeves is when people throw their trash out of cars or drop cigarette butts on the sidewalk out of pure laziness."

I'm surprised he's never been up here, but let it go. I'm not sure I want to dig too deeply. "I'm anti-litter too. Drives me crazy when people fling something in the general direction of a garbage can but don't bother to pick it up if they miss."

"Yep. Huge pet peeve." Quietly, he adds, "People shouldn't fling things."

We both know what he means by that. I can't say anything in response. My face is probably so red, it's doing the talking for me.

"What happened to you yesterday . . . well, it sucks. And it was undeserved."

I do the eyeroll-and-shrug thing. "Well, what can you do?"

I have no idea how to play this cool. It's hard enough just sitting beside him, feeling his shoulder next to mine, seeing his beat-up Adidas and the frayed hem of his jeans only inches from where my own sandals and pink-painted toes are stretched out on the gravel roof. Knowing how he sends me reeling with a kiss. Or when he tells me he thinks I'm different or that I'm brave, especially when I'm so unsure of myself.

"Whatever it is, you're doing it." He reaches over and puts his hand over mine, and on instinct I weave my fingers up through his. I suddenly wonder if that's what he meant for me to do, or if he was just trying to be reassuring in a friendly way. I relax my hand so he can pull away if he wants to without being obvious.

Instead, he tightens his fingers around mine and grins. "Hey, I have something to make you smile."

I'm about to say that having him hold my hand is enough to do it, but he lets go and turns toward his backpack. After rummaging around for a sec, he glances over his shoulder at me. "Close your eyes."

"Are you serious?"

He gives me a look that says *Get over it*, so I decide not to argue and close 'em.

I hear the zipper on his backpack as he says, "You're gonna love this. Now open."

Ten

"What?" His hands are empty. But he's grinning ear to ear. And then I see it. Right on the front of his shirt.

He put on a pocket protector. It looks out of place since it's on the pocket of a T-shirt instead of some dorky plaid button-down, but it's still hysterical.

"For me?" I say, batting my eyelashes and putting a hand over my heart.

"For you," he says. "I'll wear it all day. Just so you can see it and remind yourself to see the humor in your own situation."

"Thanks."

He settles back against the air-conditioning unit and grabs my hand. In that instant, I know I'm beyond lucky.

He glances sideways at me. "And it'll pass, you know. People will have someone or something else to talk about tomorrow, and it'll be forgotten. And anyone who knows you knows how nice you are. That whatever caused Rachel to flip out probably was a temporary thing."

"Great." Sorry, but I can't get *that* enthused on the thready hope that some other scandal will happen soon. Even if he is working hard to help me see the comical side of all of this.

"Really. No one knows why you and Rachel got so upset with each other . . . not that I know of, anyway. And I don't think anyone really cares. They just found the, um, accidental underwear thing funny. Something to talk about to get through the day. But since Margot deVries is the main one talking about it, everyone takes it with a grain of salt."

I work up the guts to look at him. "Everyone?"

"Okay, not *everyone* sees through Margot. But anyone with half a brain should. And if someone doesn't have half a brain . . . well, why would you care what they think?"

The truth is, though, I do care. "I get that," I tell him. "But even so, who wants to be the butt—pardon the pun—of everyone's jokes?"

"No one. That's human nature." His pulls our joined hands into his lap, then runs the fingers of his other hand over mine. There's a smile in his eyes that I can see even under the rim of his baseball cap. "But I've watched you with Amy, Rachel, and Kendra at WooWoo for months now. They're not going to think any differently about you in the long run. Even Rachel."

I can't help but smile at him, even as we're discussing, well, something I'd rather not. How does he do that? It's so much more than the goofy pocket protector. It's just . . . *him*.

"And about this weekend . . ."

Here goes. He's going to dump me now. He's just being nicer about it than Sean was at DIA.

"I understand if you'd rather not get together this weekend," I say quickly. "Really." It's enough to know he's supportive of me right now.

He bumps his shoulder against mine. "It's not that. I was about to say that I think you might be better off if you go out with your friends. At least this weekend. Maybe part of Rachel's problem these days is that you spent so much time with Sean Norcross? From what I could tell during your pizza parlor conversations, at least, the three of them did a lot of things without you while you were with Sean."

Even though my gut instinct is to say, *No, the fact that I like you so much is the problem*, I realize that on a deeper level, he's right. Spending time with my girlfriends right now—whether Rachel ends up coming along with us or not—is probably the best thing I can do. They need to know how important they are to me. How important they've always been to me. "You're a pretty smart guy, you know?"

He pats his T-shirt pocket. "That's why I have this."

I shake my head. He's so dorky, but so funny and so *cool* at the same time.

"We'll do something another weekend, though, if you want," he says. "Once you have things more settled with your friends. I'm not going anywhere."

I'm about to say thank you, but he leans over and kisses me. It's kind of odd, since we're sitting against the air conditioners and he's wearing both the baseball hat and his glasses, but it works for me.

Wow, does it work for me.

Entirely too soon, I hear the bell ring announcing the end of fifth period. He pulls back a few inches and says, "Well, on to the next class, I s'pose."

"Yeah." But I don't want to leave. I know if we stay, though, we'd definitely get busted, and that's the last thing I need.

What little remains of my rep would be shot for sure.

Billy stands, then pulls me up. At that moment, I hear laughter coming from the direction of the ladder and the distinct *clank* of someone climbing.

"I'd rather be gone before anyone sees us up here," I say. "Even if it is just the football players."

"Totally understood." Billy grabs my backpack and his, then pulls me toward the opposite side of the roof. "There's another ladder over here."

The gravel crunches beneath our feet and it sounds like thunder as we move over it. We get to the edge, and I realize going down is going to be way tougher than coming up. This is *high*.

"When you get to the bottom, it's not a big jump," he says. "You'll be fine. And it's behind freshman hall. No one will see us. No windows. I'll bring your backpack." He holds my hand until I'm over the edge and my foot connects with one of the rungs. He whispers for me to take my time and be careful.

I take the rungs one by one, hoping I move fast enough to keep him from being seen by whoever is coming up the other side.

Only a couple seconds after my feet connect with the ground, he's there beside me.

"Couple of football players and their friends," he says. "I saw four of them get on the roof, but they were oblivious." From his look, I can tell he's thinking the same thing I am—that getting caught being all lovey-dovey on the roof isn't something that'll help the undie incident die down.

I glance back up the ladder. "I felt like

we had to be shaking the ceiling of every classroom on the second floor, running across the roof like that."

"We probably were," he acknowledges, looking around to see if anyone's within earshot. Thankfully, we're alone here, just as he predicted. "But if anyone checks, we're not the ones who'll get caught, will we? They'll get the guys who are up there now."

"Littering," I add.

"Exactly. Want to bet five bucks on whether they get caught?"

"Not on your life."

If we want to be on time to sixth period, we have to hurry, so we both make our way around the building, heading for the closest door. He stops before opening it, reaching to loop my backpack over my arm and hike it onto my shoulder. I expect him to open the door, but he doesn't. He stands there, and his eyes look straight into mine.

I think my heart is literally going to stop.

"I meant what I said, Chloe. I'm not going anywhere. You're smart, you've got the best sense of humor, and on a lot of levels I think we see the world in the same way, even though we're very different. Do the right thing by your friends, and I'll see you tomorrow in the computer lab. Sound good?"

"Sounds good."

He gives me the softest, sweetest kiss, then opens the door and walks in ahead of me, not looking the slightest bit like a guy who nearly got caught ditching class.

I smile to myself as I hustle down the hall, heading toward chemistry and grateful I don't have to stop at my locker.

He thinks I'm smart. And funny. And now that I think about it, he didn't *once* mention a thing about me being pretty or any of that stuff.

Odd how that makes me like him that much more. How it makes me feel *normal* just to hang out with him, without any expectations or any label—like "girlfriend." I want to be so much more than just someone's girlfriend.

"Hey!"

I stop short at the familiar voice, then turn around. "Hey, Rachel."

Her eyes are bloodshot, but not so much that most people would notice. It's just that

I know her better than most people. "I just saw you coming from freshman hall . . . were you, um, skipping class?"

Will she turn me in if I say yes?

I did promise her I'd always tell her the truth.

Keeping my voice low enough so no one else can hear me, I say, "Busted. I needed to get out of here for a little while."

"Me too." She looks down for a sec, apparently embarrassed to admit it. "I stayed home this morning. Faked a headache." She glances behind her, like she's afraid someone's watching her, then looks back at me. "Um, are you doing anything after cross-country? 'Cause if you're not, I was hoping you could come over for a while. Or go out. Whatever you want."

I can see in her face that she expects me to make an excuse. That she wants to apologize but is afraid I won't give her the chance. "I'll be there," I tell her. "Whatever you want."

After I spend cross-country working on getting Eric to ask Amy out.

Rachel nods, then starts to walk by me on her way to class. Just as she passes me, though, she turns around. "I saw Billy walking by right before I saw you. Did you notice he's wearing Ass Grab Pants today?" She smiles as big as I've seen her smile in a long time. "I didn't think Geek Boy had it in him."

"Yeah, I noticed."

"Good." She leans in and gives me a hug. "See you after cross-country?"

"Absolutely."

And I know everything will work out. For all of us.

truth or dare

By the bestselling author of the Mates, Dates series,

Cathy Hopkins

Meet Cat, Becca, Squidge, Mac, and Lia. These girls and guys
are totally tight—and totally obsessed with the game of truth or
dare . . . even when it reveals too much!

Every book is a different dare . . . and a fun new adventure.

Read them all:

White Lies and Barefaced Truths

The Princess of Pop

Teen Queens and Has-Beens

Starstruck

Double Dare

From Simon Pulse
Published by Simon & Schuster

Ella (Mental) Watson is a rules girl, always on hand to offer impeccable advice. But when life gets complicated, will the rules go out the window?

From Simon Pulse
Published by Simon & Schuster